Christmas
on the
Coast

Christmas
on the
Coast

REBECCA BOXALL

LAKE UNION
PUBLISHING

Text copyright © 2017 by Rebecca Boxall
All rights reserved.

Published by Lake Union Publishing, Seattle

www.apub.com

Amazon, the Amazon logo, and Lake Union Publishing are trademarks of Amazon.com, Inc., or its affiliates.

ISBN-13: 9781542047005
ISBN-10: 1542047005

Cover design by @blacksheep-uk.com

Map illustration by David Woodroffe

Printed in the United States of America

*In memory of my grandparents and
the first little dot (2010)
And for my mum and siblings*

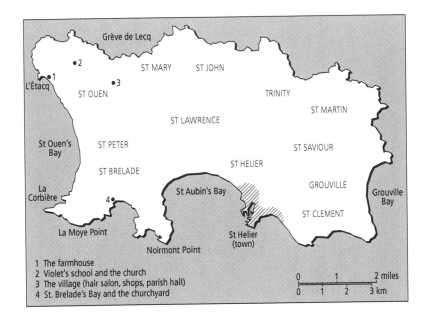

Grève de Lecq

•2   ST MARY   ST JOHN
•1
L'Étacq   •3
ST OUEN   TRINITY
                                        ST MARTIN
            ST LAWRENCE

St Ouen's   ST PETER   ST SAVIOUR
Bay
            ST BRELADE   ST HELIER

La   GROUVILLE
Corbière   4•   St Aubin's Bay   Grouville
                                                             Bay
                                        ST CLEMENT
La Moye Point   St Helier
                               (town)
            Noirmont Point

1 The farmhouse
2 Violet's school and the church
3 The village (hair salon, shops, parish hall)   0   1   2 miles
4 St. Brelade's Bay and the churchyard   0   1   2   3 km

Preface

Jersey is one of a handful of tiny islands that make up the Channel Islands in the English Channel. Though it has an allegiance to the British Crown, it has its own government and independence and is geographically closer to France than England. This made it extremely vulnerable during the Second World War once the German forces had occupied France in the early summer of 1940. Jersey was invaded on 1 July 1940 and remained under Nazi rule for five long, hard years until its liberation in May 1945. Occupying the Channel Islands was a great coup for Hitler – it was the closest he came to his greatest desire: to invade and conquer Britain. For the government of Jersey at the time – who were required to bring into effect all German orders – it was extremely difficult. And for those civilians living under occupation it was a time of great hardship. Much like during the blitz in London, it brought out the very best human spirit in many and created a great sense of solidarity. But inevitably there were also conflicts within the community, causing grudges and grievances between families that, in some cases, continue to this day. Queenie's journal in this novel is entirely fictional, though it is based upon historical research.

PART ONE

'WHAT IS THIS LIFE IF, FULL OF CARE,

WE HAVE NO TIME TO STAND AND STARE?'

From 'Leisure'
By W. H. Davies

Chapter One

Jersey, December 2016

Liberty

'I'm sorry, madam, but you can't park there.'

Libby turned off the Volvo's engine and emerged brazenly from the car, deciding to pretend she was slightly hard of hearing. The wind howling onshore from the Atlantic was loud enough to give her a good excuse at any rate.

'I said you can't park there!' the nasal voice tried again, louder. Libby sighed. She was no good at brazen. Her friend Stella was so much better at it.

She turned around. 'But the supermarket car park's full,' she said, smiling. 'What do you suggest I do?'

'There's another car park just down the road,' said the man. He was tiny, swamped by his luminous jacket, with greasy hair and a Freddie Mercury moustache.

'But that's miles away! I'll have to lug all my shopping with me!'

'Sorry, madam,' he repeated, ushering her back towards the car in an officious manner.

'Damn traffic wardens,' Libby muttered defiantly, though quietly enough that the warden wouldn't hear. She got back into the driving seat and considered moving the car. Then she realised the little man had disappeared. Taking a leaf out of Stella's book, she left the car where it was and legged it round the shop, relieved on her return to find she hadn't been landed with a parking ticket. Her heart was hammering in protest at this rebellious behaviour. She was a police officer, for goodness sake. She wasn't *meant* to be disobedient.

And the truth was, she was the very opposite of rebellious: an anxious people-pleaser with several roles to play – police officer, vicar's wife, mother of three highly demanding children. Libby had teetered throughout the larger part of her forty-eight years on the edge of a bottomless pit of angst and worry, her brain picking at recurring neuroses as though choosing cards from a well-worn pack, and it was usually Stella she relied on in times of stress. The two of them had been best friends since primary school and had been through thick and thin together, reuniting at the same university after an enforced three years apart and then starting their police training in London. They even celebrated a 'friend anniversary' – or 'franniversary', as Stella called it. Over two decades ago, they'd decided to start celebrating the day their friendship had been born: the reception year Christmas party at the end of term, when Stella had got into a terrible scrap with another child who'd stolen her cracker and Libby had saved the day by giving Stella her own.

It was just like a wedding anniversary or a birthday and every year they tried to think of something more unusual to do together in its honour: one year they'd braved a tandem parachute jump; another time they'd taken part in a parade through town dressed as Christmas elves. This year they were going to learn how to make Jersey Wonders and give baskets of these local doughy bakes, similar to doughnuts, to the Women's Refuge on Christmas Day – one of the charities Stella was passionate about. She always tried to think of ways to help local charities, especially around Christmastime.

Libby was just about to check the date of their baking lesson on her phone (the timing would depend on the tide as, by tradition, Wonders had to be made as the tide went out) when she clocked the traffic warden heading towards the car with a look of fury on his face.

'Argh!' She dropped the phone and started the engine, speeding out of the dodgy parking space and finding herself breathless with anxiety as she spotted the man running behind the car and waving his arms about in protest.

It was only when she was sure she'd shaken him off that Libby hastily inhaled some oxygen. She really must learn to control her breathing better. Everyone these days seemed to think mindful breathing was the answer to everything but Libby wasn't sure she ever managed to do it right. She always ended up feeling like she was hyperventilating whenever she tried it. She checked the clock on her dashboard. Midday already. Damn. She only had an hour until she was meeting Amy in town – an hour in which to race back to the Vicarage in L'Etacq, unload the shopping, swap her skinny jeans and nautical top for a nice dress and pray like mad she'd be able to park near the wedding-dress shop. She just didn't have the heart for more illegal parking.

Unfortunately, her decision to park legally meant that instead of arriving at the boutique looking like a calm and composed mother-of-the-bride-to-be, Libby turned up puce in the face, sweat trickling uncomfortably down her back, having jogged all the way from the multistorey car park at Minden Place. As she burst through the door she was greeted with a frown from her highly organised and competent daughter and a barely concealed sneer from the snooty shop owner.

Libby had a flashback to her favourite film, *Pretty Woman*, and longed to undergo a miraculous transformation into Julia Roberts in the scene where she swaggers back into the shop laden with bags to confront the snooty saleswoman who'd previously snubbed her.

Amy's high-pitched voice cut into her fantasy. 'Mum, I've only got forty minutes till I need to be back at work. You don't even work on

Fridays. Why are you always late?' Amy didn't wait for an answer. She was a high-flying lawyer and high-flying lawyers didn't have time for the kind of lame excuse Libby was bound to provide.

'Now, I've narrowed it down to this, this and this,' Amy said, holding up three different gowns for her mother's perusal. Libby felt a little hurt that Amy hadn't invited her to the very first trying-on session a week earlier, but she couldn't help but smile when she saw the dresses, instinctively reaching out to feel the silky satin material, then quickly pulling back her hand when she saw the shop owner step forwards in a proprietary manner.

'Gosh, well, they're all lovely,' she said, and she meant it, though she couldn't help thinking they were all a bit *stiff*. A dress hanging on the rail to her left suddenly caught her attention – white lace, long sleeves; it looked like it would swish beautifully up and down the aisle. 'Oh, what about this?' she suggested.

'Mum, I've been through this once already. I'm not trying on anything else. *This* is the shortlist. Now, I'm thinking this one,' Amy said. 'Let me try it on.'

Libby followed Amy through to the posh changing room and sat on a low-seated chair, waiting for her daughter. Unfortunately, here she came face to face with her own reflection: some horrible sadist (the shop owner, presumably) had thought to leave the brides' mothers with only a mirror to look at while they waited for their glamorous daughters to appear.

In truth, Libby didn't look *that* bad. In some ways, she and Amy weren't dissimilar-looking – both olive-skinned and leggy, with dark, bobbed hair and hazel eyes flecked with green. But while Amy had youth on her side and an enviably flat stomach, Libby had dark circles under her eyes and noticeably grey roots (she really must book herself in at the hairdresser's). Worst of all, her midriff didn't bear close – or, for that matter, far – inspection after she'd developed a role for herself as a human dustbin for the food she'd unfailingly prepared and that her children had unfailingly played with and then left at mealtimes over the years.

'What do you think?' asked Amy, for once sounding a little unsure of herself.

'Stunning,' Libby replied with a wide smile. The dress was an ivory-coloured sheath with no shape or detail and was a little simple and business-like for her own tastes, but Libby knew Amy would look gorgeous in any one of the dresses in the shop. 'You must get that one!' Libby told her and – composure fully recovered – Amy embraced her mother in her rather brisk way and looked at her watch.

'Thanks, Mum. Now I'd better get back to the office.'

'Oh, come on, darling, how about lunch? I'm meeting Stella. We're going to Seagulls.'

Amy hesitated. Libby knew it was Amy's favourite restaurant in town. Libby thought it was a bit fancy, with tiny, artistic-looking plates of food served in frothy bubbles that reminded her of washing-up suds, but she'd booked it in the hope her daughter might for once grace Libby with her presence.

'Did you get a table by the window?' Amy asked.

'Of course!'

'Well, okay then, but I'll have to ring my PA and get her to push back my meeting. And I can only stay an hour.'

Libby felt pathetically grateful, even though she'd be the one footing the bill. With Amy's phone call dealt with, they reached the restaurant and Libby watched Amy's spirits visibly soar as she was treated with great deference by the attentive waiting staff.

'Please, this way, Miss Amy,' a squat, hairy man said as he took the two of them to the best table in the restaurant, with views overlooking the harbour and row upon row of gleaming white yachts. The tinted window was slightly open and Libby caught a waft of briny air and heard the raucous squawk of the gulls that had inspired the establishment's name.

'Here I am!' came a familiar noisy voice a moment later, making Libby smile. Stella came bounding towards them, her strawberry blonde curls bouncing around her wide face and her voluminous outfit flapping. Stella was large – not exactly fat, but tall and always wearing loose, bohemian clothes that made her seem bigger than she actually was. It was all part of her charm. She didn't care about staying slim or getting slim or looking slim. She was who she was. Appearances were unimportant to her, though she was always interested in seeing other people's purchases after a shopping spree.

'Where's the dress, then?' she asked Amy immediately, looking around for shopping bags while an obsequious waiter served the champagne Libby had optimistically pre-ordered as a special treat for Amy.

'Oh, it's not with me,' Amy laughed, taking a dainty sip of her drink. 'It's being altered. I was just trying on dresses to get a general idea.'

'Ha! Should've guessed,' Stella chuckled. 'Our Amy isn't going to be getting married in any old thing. Has your mum ever told you what I wore on my wedding day? Not that the marriage ended well, as you know. Probably all down to the dress.'

'Oh my goodness,' Libby snorted. 'The one you wore in the end was an old bridesmaid's dress you had hanging in your cupboard. It wasn't *that* bad but the one you *were* going to wear was hideous! Honestly, Amy, you should have seen her. She'd found this old frock in her mum's wardrobe, dating back to the war. It was made out of a pair of curtains! When Sybil saw her daughter in that, she nearly fainted. Said the pantomime dame had worn it in some wartime production of *Cinderella*. She couldn't remember why she had it. I think she burned it after that.'

'I thought it was rather nice! Though it did smell a bit. Male body odour!' Stella said, guffawing with laughter. 'Cheers, anyway!' she added, clinking her glass against Libby's and Amy's with such force they spilt some of the precious champagne. 'Now, on to more serious matters. Amy, you're starting to behave like a bridezilla. You've got to stop giving your mum such a hard time.'

Libby felt her body tense and instantly wanted to crawl under a stone. Stella was marvellously protective but sometimes her brutal honesty wasn't exactly helpful. Amy was as prickly as a blackberry bush at the best of times. She saw Amy bristle but then, instead of arguing back, her daughter slowly smiled.

'You're right, as always,' she said to Stella. 'I need to take a chill pill. My friend Bethany's getting married, too. That's the trouble. It's become competitive.'

'Aha! Bride wars! Tell me more!'

Stella loved a good story, especially if it involved conflict. Libby took another sip of champagne and decided, for once in her life, to relax.

The meal over, and having restricted herself to just one small glass of bubbly (Stella had drunk almost all of the bottle, making the most of a day off), Libby headed off to collect Milo from school as she always did on Fridays, though she was certain her son would rather take the bus as he did Monday to Thursday.

'How was your day, darling?' Libby asked as Milo climbed into the passenger seat with a face like thunder. He had the same colouring and hazel eyes as Libby and Amy but he was going through a spotty phase and the poor boy was angry if anyone so much as looked at him, clearly wishing he could walk around with a bag over his head.

'Fine,' he mumbled.

'What was the *best* thing that happened?' Libby tried, recalling a parenting class she'd attended years ago that had offered advice on how to achieve slightly more interesting answers from your child.

Milo grunted, not gracing this question with an answer.

'Did you have Art today?' Libby tried instead, knowing it was Milo's favourite subject, but Milo just pointedly shoved in his earphones. He turned away from his mother to stare grumpily out of the window.

Libby gave up and switched on the radio. Milo's interests these days were fairly limited. Unless you were prepared to talk to him about drumming, Chelsea (his girlfriend, not the football club) or computers, he wasn't prepared to engage in any conversation whatsoever. He communicated quite well with looks, though, glowering at his mother in a way that suggested he could barely tolerate her. *How did my chubby, cheeky baby turn into this sullen teenager?* she wondered for the umpteenth time.

As soon as they arrived home Milo vanished to his room, the sound of drums striking up two minutes later, while Libby set about making shepherd's pie in the long and narrow kitchen. It was a fine evening and the sun was pouring in through the end window, casting a homely glow over the pine kitchen table. She left the onions to their own devices for a moment and went to stand and peer at the view.

Libby longed to own a house but, like army families, vicars and their loved ones lived where they were placed and never had the security of their own bricks and mortar. And she had to admit that, despite the fact that the Vicarage was rather bland and box-like, she and Henry would never have been able to afford to live in a place with such views in ordinary circumstances. From the kitchen window she could see a patchwork of potato fields leading down to St Ouen's Bay, sweeping from Faulkner Fisheries at one end (nestled inside an old German bunker from the Second World War) to Corbière lighthouse at the other. Until recently the lighthouse had blared its foghorn all through the night in misty weather until the powers-that-be decided it was an unnecessary extra in this age of more sophisticated navigation aids. As a child, she'd always found the sound of the horn blaring through the night strangely comforting.

Libby smiled as she thought back to her childhood in a farmhouse just down the road from the Vicarage – her father had inherited it early as his mother and aunt had set up home elsewhere with their husbands, though the farmland itself had been sold off by Libby's great-grandfather long before they took possession of the house. She'd been fifteen when disaster struck after her father fell victim to a Ponzi scheme, losing his life's savings and necessitating the sale of their much-loved family home. Her parents had decided to make a fresh start in Canterbury, where Libby's mother was from, and where property prices were more affordable. It had meant leaving behind the home, island and friends Libby had adored – most especially Stella – which was particularly hard as an only child who had no idea that fate would return her to Jersey just a few years later when she met Henry. Understanding the reasons for the move, she hadn't wanted to make a fuss, and so she'd gone along with it all with a smile on her face. Her brain, though, hadn't been tricked and had rewarded her with a lifetime of low-level anxiety that flared up whenever she started to overload herself, however much she told herself she didn't have a good enough reason for it.

Libby was stirred from her reverie by the shrill of the telephone. She grabbed the handset, then returned to the hob to save the onions.

'Vicarage,' she answered.

'Libby, it's your dad.'

'Dad! How funny, I was just thinking about you. Gosh, it's not often you call. It's usually Mum. Is everything okay?'

'Don't worry unduly, but your mum's had a little accident. She's sprained her wrist rather badly. Fell off a stool when she was dusting! She told me in no uncertain terms not to tell you about it. She knows you'll be straight over to Canterbury and she doesn't want to pile on more pressure when you're so busy, but I knew you'd want to know.'

'Poor Mum! Can I talk to her?'

'She's just having a little lie-down. She's in shock, I think. It scared her more than anything. An unwelcome reminder of her advancing years.'

'Look, I must come over. She's so house-proud and – sorry Dad, but I know I can be honest with you – you won't manage to keep things up to her usual standard. I'll just come for a week – maybe next Friday? The sixteenth? – and help her get ready for Christmas as well. I know she likes to have everything bought and wrapped nice and early!'

Libby's father laughed. 'You're right, I'm already in trouble for cutting corners. But are you sure you can manage it?'

'Of course!' Libby said, already calculating what she'd need to do to get everything in order before she could abandon ship in Jersey. First things first, she needed to tell the family.

Libby had expected it to be just the three of them for supper once Henry had returned from his 'visits' – he was a vicar of the sociable variety, generally doing his rounds in the parish at drink o'clock. But with Henry safely home and sitting with Milo at the table in the kitchen, the back door slammed just as she was serving up the shepherd's pie.

Libby felt her heart swoop as her middle child entered the kitchen from the utility room, his blond curls dishevelled and his suit all crumpled. This was a habitual swoop born of the extreme mood swings her son seemed to suffer from: it always took her a nerve-jangling thirty seconds to gauge which kind of person he'd be today. The happy, effervescing Liam or the exhausted and needy Liam who – though he rented his own flat – often appeared at the Vicarage after a day working at the bank. She held her breath, then released it again when she saw her son return her grin, his twinkly blue eyes shining. Happy Liam. Happy Liam made for a happy evening.

'Darling!' she said. 'Do you want supper? Or are you still vegetarian?'

'No. I managed three days of that! Yes please to supper but I'm not drinking. I've brought a green juice with me.'

'Are you sure? I've just opened a lovely red,' Henry said from the end of the table, proffering it towards his son like a wine waiter.

Liam looked a bit tempted, but this was clearly his latest fad. Her son was not only extreme in his moods but also in his lifestyle – one minute he was running marathons and existing on rabbit food, the next he was indulging in way too much alcohol and a veritable smorgasbord of recreational drugs. Henry didn't know this, but Liam was gratifyingly close to Libby and told her everything – much of which she often wished she didn't know.

With nearly all her family present, Libby decided this was the moment to tell them about her mother.

'I need to tell you something,' she said, seizing on a conversational pause.

'Oh yes?' replied Henry, smiling benignly.

'I'm going away.'

'Away?' asked Henry, laughing slightly as though Libby had cracked a joke. It was understandable, in a way. She'd only spent a handful of nights away on her own since she'd first had Amy twenty-five years ago.

'Yes,' she said, taking a sip of wine.

'But how long for?'

'Just a week.'

'What? When do you go? And where? And why?' Henry asked, now looking a little worried. Disloyally, she imagined it was because he knew he'd have to feed himself and take on her share of the chores and arrangements to do with Milo instead of prioritising his job.

'I leave at the end of next week,' Libby said. 'I'm going to Canterbury. Dad rang earlier. Apparently Mum's had a fall and sprained her wrist quite badly. She can't do any of the household chores and you know what a perfectionist she is. And anyway, I've been meaning to visit them for ages; they're not getting any younger.'

'You're a saint,' Henry said. 'But don't go and overdo it over there. Try to treat it as a break for yourself. You need one,' he added, displaying a rare moment of insight. Libby felt herself soften towards him but then he ruined it. 'Oh, heavens!' he exclaimed. 'I've forgotten choir practice!' He stood up, still wolfing down the remainder of his shepherd's pie.

'But choir isn't on this week!' Libby said, silently resenting the churchly interruption that had become such an unwelcome part of her life and marriage. She'd had no idea when Henry had proposed to her all those years ago that his job as a vicar was not, in fact, a job, but an all-consuming vocation.

'There was a change of plan. I promised the new organist I'd be there. I'll be back as soon as I can! Save me some wine! And pud!'

'Stupid vicar job,' Libby muttered to herself as she cleared the plates. Milo immediately darted off upstairs to play his drums while Liam followed her through to the kitchen to tell her all about the latest money-spinning idea he'd had that he was sure would be the one to extricate him from his banking job. With a huge effort, Libby smiled and made encouraging-sounding noises.

'Honestly, Mum, I guarantee you that by this time next year I'll be a millionaire! I'll buy you a house!'

Libby straightened from stacking the dishwasher and turned to her son. When he was in a sunny, optimistic mood, Liam's smile was so innocent it hurt to look at it. She hugged him, fighting back tears. 'Any house I want?' she asked.

'Any! One of those cod houses you like, maybe?'

They both knew an enviable nineteenth-century cod house would never be within reach of either of them but Libby played along with Liam's little fantasy.

'With a swimming pool?'

'But of course!'

'Liam . . . darling, you're okay, aren't you?'

'Happy as Larry!'

'Only . . . I don't know. One minute you're full of beans, then you're overdoing the partying, then horribly down in the dumps. Do you think . . . ? I just wonder if you should see someone. A doctor?'

But Liam just laughed and rubbed his mother's back. 'I'm fine, Mum. One hundred per cent. I promise.'

Libby looked at her son but when he was in an 'up' mood, Liam simply couldn't see that his behaviour was a concern. There was only one thing she could do: store that particular card back in her pack of worries.

Chapter Two

Jersey, November 1941

Queenie's journal

It seems a little bit daft to start keeping a diary at the end of the year instead of at the beginning of a new one and I've no idea how long I'll manage to keep it up for, but I've promised myself to keep a daily record at least until the year's end: my Christmas journal. I wish I'd started to write it in July last year when we were first invaded. My goodness, that was a shock. Jersey was still being advertised as the perfect place for a wartime holiday that spring and then all of a sudden, at the end of June, there was an absolutely terrifying air raid, even though the island was undefended. Apparently no one had told the Germans! They dropped leaflets after that, telling us that if we waved white flags from all the buildings they wouldn't continue their attack. Well, we didn't want anyone else to be killed or injured and there was no army to defend us, so what could we do? Though I made sure to wave a pair of white bloomers, rather than a flag, as a small gesture of rebellion.

It was something Papa said at the table last night that made me pick up this notebook and pencil this evening.

'We're living through history right now,' he said, helping himself to a hunk of homemade bread with his beefy farmer's hands. We were eating the vegetable soup Mama prepares nearly every night now. We all keep promising her it's delicious but in truth it's just so dreadfully *boring*.

I should add, I've decided that if I'm going to keep a journal I might as well be truthful – otherwise what's the point? I must be careful though. If the German soldiers come across it, I dread to think of the consequences. I'm going to hide it under the floorboards, where I hid my wireless when the Germans first told us there was a ban on listening to BBC radio. They didn't actually confiscate our sets in the end but my sweetheart, Albert, gave mine to me for my eighteenth birthday and I was blowed if I was going to risk letting the officials get their grubby paws on such a precious gift.

The Germans have lifted the ban for now but Papa thinks they're likely to confiscate everyone's wirelesses soon and he's worried the penalties for hiding them will be very severe. But we *need* the BBC news bulletins – how are we meant to know how the war's going without them? I suppose that's the point . . .

Anyway, Papa made me realise that although life has become so narrow and tedious and cold and hard, one day someone might actually be interested in reading what it was like living on a tiny British island taken over by the Germans. So I shall try to write the journal as if for a stranger who knows nothing about me. In fact, perhaps I should start by describing where I live: a farm that's been passed down Papa's family for generations. All four of my grandparents lived with us until recently but they died, one by one, in the space of a couple of years. Mamie, whose mother was a ballerina from Moscow, was the last to leave us. She was my favourite: she adored hats and every time I went into town she used to beg me to bring her back another one from her favourite milliner's. Papa says it's just as well they don't have to live through this bleak period in time but I still miss Mamie terribly . . .

The farmhouse is a sturdy building right beside the sea in a place called L'Etacq (the *cueillette* of Millais) in the parish of St Ouen, tucked into the north-west corner of an island nine miles wide and five miles long.

From the window on the landing I can see the ancient Rocco Tower, built on a rocky outcrop off St Ouen's Bay, and behind that the gleaming white lighthouse at Corbière – no longer permitted to cast out its life-saving beam at night. I've often fantasised about living in both these landmarks, cut off from land by the tide for several hours every day. I love company, don't get me wrong, but I relish my solitude, too, and I don't get much time to myself as a rule.

Aside from a couple of small shops, there's nothing in L'Etacq apart from farmhouses, steep potato fields that merge into the gorse-covered cliffs, the Atlantic Ocean and mile upon mile of butter-coloured beach. We're only a short hop to St Ouen's village, though, and there's a little more going on there: the parish hall, a hair salon and a few more shops, including a butcher's, two bakeries and a couple of others selling 'all sorts', as Mama says.

Before the war, Jersey was like paradise on earth and we're all hanging on to the hope that it will be again. Writing those words just then, I felt an icy shiver run through me. And not from the north wind rattling through the farmhouse: I'm tucked under two thick eiderdowns beside Noelle who, as usual, has fallen asleep instantly. Such a docile creature, my younger sister: a true sleeping beauty.

A shiver of fear at the thought that we might not win this war. It's a question I want to ask every day: if we don't, what will happen to us then? They're already talking about introducing compulsory German lessons in the schools. Will we all be fluent German speakers, forever abiding by a set of – honestly quite ridiculous – rules dictated to us by these sinister leaders we hardly dare discuss? I must stop this train of thought. Papa would have kittens if he were to read these defeatist musings. We must never give up. 'One day, we will be liberated,' Papa said last night. Dear God, I hope he's right.

Chapter Three

Jersey, December 2016

Liberty

Saturday dawned cold and bright. While Henry snored away beside her, Libby lay in bed thinking about all the chores she needed to accomplish before she set up the church hall for the parish Christmas market that was taking place in the afternoon. Washing. Ironing. Labelling Milo's clothes for his field trip after Christmas. Boring, boring, boring. Her phone beeped and she reached for it immediately. A text from Stella.

Fancy an open viewing this morning? I'm on a late today. L'arc en Ciel on Chemin du Moulin! Next to the honesty stall selling eggs and veggies. Tempted?

Libby was. Sorely. She'd walked past that house a thousand times and it was a corker. Sod the chores.

What time? she replied.

Ten. Meet you there?

Will do! I'll bring the coffee today. She added a smiley face. She was quite *into* smiley faces since Amy had shown her how to do them, though she hadn't yet graduated to all the other fancy emojis.

Two hours later, and with most of her chores completed in a rushed frenzy, Libby arrived at the open viewing, leaving the flask of coffee and the biscuits in the car. Neither Libby nor Stella was actually in a position to buy a house. Libby had the Vicarage until Henry retired and Stella was extremely happy in her one-bedroom cottage on the five-mile road in St Ouen, just five minutes from the Vicarage in L'Etacq. But there was nothing they enjoyed more than meeting each other at an open viewing and having a good nose around places that were on the market, then drinking their coffee in the car afterwards while they analysed the way each particular house had been dressed or extended or neglected.

'Where's Rusty?' Libby asked Stella as they ambled up the driveway of the vast mansion, Stella adorned in a kaftan and Birkenstocks in honour of the sunny weather, never mind that it was eight degrees and Libby was snuggled up in a parka. Rusty was Stella's dog – a mongrel she'd saved when she'd found him caught up in the middle of a domestic violence case – and he usually accompanied them on their house viewings, enjoying a nose around the gardens just as much as Libby and Stella relished their inspections of the interiors.

'He's knackered. Took him for a massive walk this morning so he declined to escort us today. Uh-oh, it's that estate agent again. The one with the spiky hair and the muscles. Gavin.'

'Oh damn, we'd better go. He gave us a right telling off at that last viewing for being time-wasters.' Libby turned to head back to the car.

'Not so fast! We'll just go round to the back. There are loads of people here today. We'll just avoid him.'

'Really? But Stella, I hate being told off!'

'Wimp! Come on, what's he going to do? Call the police?' Stella chuckled at this and grabbed hold of Libby, dragging her round to the back of the house.

It was immediately obvious that the place was spectacular. Even the back porch was immaculate. The entire place had been Farrow & Balled to within an inch of its life – all soft greys and greens, 'Elephant's Breath' and 'Cooking Apple Green' – and the kitchen was to die for.

'An Aga, of course,' remarked Libby as she clocked the navy blue range snugly fitted amidst the sleek granite worktops and directly opposite the vast island on which there were no piles of admin, or anything that would indicate anyone actually lived in the house – just a glass vase filled with a divine display of tasteful flowers (none of your bog-standard carnations here, thank you very much). The grey and green theme continued throughout, to the point where it might have got a little dull were it not for the clever touches of 'brights' that had been introduced here and there: shocking pink velvet cushions neatly plumped on the dove-grey sofas; rose-gold mosaic tiles in the bathrooms; one wall in the master bedroom papered with an exquisite turquoise and silver wallpaper decorated with birds, setting off the simplicity of the rest of the room.

As well, everywhere had been dressed for Christmas, and it was this that took their wonder to new levels. White fairy lights had been woven into the very fabric of the house, twinkling with contentment; tasteful, neutral-coloured letters spelling out 'PEACE' and 'CHRISTMAS' had been discreetly placed on the mantelpiece above the roaring fire; and the entrance hall housed a six-foot Christmas tree, so artfully decorated Libby was beginning to suspect an interior designer had been employed for the job.

'That smell!' groaned Stella as they inhaled the distinctive pine scent. 'Oh balls, here comes your man. Quick, behind the tree!' Stella grabbed hold of Libby and, from their hidden position, they spotted Gavin swagger into the hall, walking strangely like a caveman. He was heavily engrossed in conversation with a smart-looking older couple, both wearing blazers. The lady had neatly coiffed white hair and her husband, also with neat white hair, cleared his throat a lot.

'I can see this marvellous place is ticking all your boxes,' said Gavin with a faux posh accent and Libby and Stella rolled their eyes at each other.

'A fiver says he'll mention the "wow factor" in the next two minutes,' whispered Stella.

'Just you wait until you see the kitchen,' said Gavin, taking care over his vowels. 'It's really got the wow factor!'

Libby snorted loudly.

'Hello?' Gavin asked in a suspicious voice, approaching the tree.

Libby and Stella tried to hide themselves better. 'Budge over, he's going to see me,' Libby whispered.

'I can't!' Stella cried, just as the tree began to topple. The two of them watched in horror as it crashed to the ground, the sound of crunching baubles like firing bullets.

'What the . . . ?' spluttered Gavin. 'You're kiddin' me! You two again! I thought I told you I didn't want to see your bleedin' faces ever again!' His accent had gone from faux posh to rough in a millisecond. The smart couple took a step back, alarmed, while Libby and Stella prepared themselves to run. Gavin looked at them, then at his retreating potential customers, in an obvious dilemma about which couple to follow.

'Leg it!' Stella shouted, capitalising on his hesitation. She and Libby hurled themselves past the devastation and out of the front door, weaving around various stunned-looking couples, and jumped into their respective cars. They drove, both knowing exactly where to meet – down at the site of the old Milano Bars where, if the house viewing was in St Ouen, they always took their coffee. Now no more than a car park, the beachside location could win prizes for its views of the Bay and elderly couples often parked up there at high tide and nodded off, lulled to sleep by the lap of the sea. They pulled up next to each other. Stella got out of her car and quickly hopped into Libby's. They looked at each other, both still breathless, then collapsed into laughter.

'Oh my goodness! Gavin! Seriously, we can't ever go to a viewing if it's his firm again. He really will get us arrested,' Libby hiccuped. 'But I do feel bad about the tree. It was beautiful. All those decorations! We'll have to do something.'

'I know, it was funny but also terrible! How much have you got on you?'

Libby looked in her purse. 'Twenty?'

'Give me that, then, and I'll put in forty. Sixty quid ought to buy them a new load of posh decorations. I'm sure the tree will have survived.'

'But how will you get the money to them? Just stick it through the letter box?'

'No, Libby, that would be weedy. I'll wait until the viewing's over, then go and see the people who own it and grovel to them. Now, that's enough excitement for one day. You need to get back and set up for the Christmas market!'

'I do,' agreed Libby, wiping tears of laughter from her eyes. 'But thank you! That was a real tonic, having a good laugh. What would I do without you?'

'You'd survive!' Stella said with a grin. 'Let me have a quick slurp of coffee, then I'll be off.'

After a Sunday filled with churchly activity – the Christmas market, although festive, was a real slog for the organisers – Libby finally sat down in the evening and consulted her list of everything she needed to accomplish before heading off to Canterbury. She tried to quell the mounting panic. The list now covered two A4 pages and she had only four days – workdays at that – within which to achieve everything on it. There was only one thing for it. She set her alarm for five on Monday morning.

The following day, barely awake, she began chopping onions, preparing two different types of casserole and a Bolognese for the freezer.

Henry was perfectly capable of producing a meal if he put his mind to it but the guilt she felt at abandoning her family would only be assuaged by a freezer full of home-cooked meals. Four hours later, she arrived at work and, as always, she felt momentarily relieved to be able to sit in her office chair for a few moments, collect herself, and then make a cup of tea before dealing with the pile of papers on her desk. After years in the force – with Stella beside her all the way – she'd worked her way up to detective sergeant. But five years ago, she'd ducked out of the high stress of the Drugs Squad for a secondment to a law firm specialising in fighting financial crime, something she was particularly passionate about after her own family's experience at the hands of fraudsters. It was very different now, working in an office with lawyers, and her greatest joy was that she no longer had to work shifts.

Libby checked her boss's diary to see when he might be free. She needed to request a week's worth of annual leave, starting the following week. She had plenty of holiday left over as the family hadn't been away this year; she just hoped she'd be allowed to take it at such short notice. Her tea savoured and Farty's diary ostensibly clear, she went through to his office. No sign of him. Perhaps it was a little early still. Ideal. She should have time to print off the carol service sheets for Henry before Farty arrived. Her boss was actually called Arty – an abbreviation of Arthur – but of course he'd been foisted with the inevitable nickname. He was perfectly nice, poor man, and didn't deserve such a name, though he probably wouldn't have cared even if he were aware of it: he was a thick-skinned sort of person, rather military in both his approach and appearance: smart, short and proud, with a bristling moustache.

Libby stood nervously at the printer, darting guilty looks at her colleagues as they passed her on their way to the kitchen. *Come on, come on*, she silently willed the machine, which – *Oh hell, it just would, wouldn't it?* – suddenly jammed mid-printing.

'Gone wrong again?' asked Glenda. Dear Glenda. She was ever so sweet and terribly unfortunate-looking: bucked teeth, florid skin knitted with spider veins, bottle-top glasses and thick, bobbly cardigans. But she was also just a *teeny* bit on the nosy side. 'Can I help at all?' she added, reaching towards the paper-munching monster, but Libby tried to head her off at the pass. Glenda was hardly an expert in technology. Any training session the office had to endure was rendered hellish as Glenda painfully asked the long-suffering trainer to explain *just one more time* how to open a document or close a document or something equally straightforward. Glenda was clearly just itching to know what Libby was printing.

'Don't worry, all under control,' Libby assured her with a strained smile.

'If you're sure . . .' said Glenda, hovering.

'Absolutely,' Libby replied as she clocked Farty coming through the main entrance. Damn. The air con in the office was known for its sub-zero setting but Libby felt her body temperature rising and her face flushing as she pulled helplessly at the wretched service sheets, ripping them and only adding to the problem.

'Here, let me,' offered Sam, the office hunk, as he parked his coffee cup on a nearby cabinet and expertly retrieved the chewed-up documents, swiftly cleaning up the whole debacle with several neat and dexterous movements. He didn't even seem to notice the documents contained the lyrics to 'Away in a Manger' instead of detailing some appalling fraud or other. He passed the copies to Libby with a smile and she caught a waft of his fresh and lemony aftershave. For a moment, she felt like she might fall head first in love with him – right there and then – for rescuing her. But then she saw sense: he was about twenty years younger than her and had floppy hair (a pet hate). *And*, of course, she was married! Still, it was terribly kind of him.

'Thank you,' she squeaked as she belted back to her desk and stuffed the carol sheets into her handbag before kicking it under the desk. *Bloody Henry*, she thought to herself. *Why can't he just bloody well buy a printer? How does he think most vicars manage? In fact, how on earth will he cope while I'm away? True, Milo's got that little second-hand one for printing off essays, but it won't be any good for bulk printing. And there are so many services next week; so many service sheets! NOT MY PROBLEM!* Libby shouted inwardly at herself so she wouldn't spin into a complete state and end up cancelling her flight.

The next moment, Farty was at her desk, standing over her and gently swaying back and forth as though he were on a ship. 'Ah, there you are . . . Libby, we've got a big case coming in next week. I'm going to need you to do some digging for us.'

'Oh gosh, Far . . . Arty, I'm so sorry but I don't think I'm going to be able to help. I really need to take some holiday. It's my mother . . .'

Farty frowned. Libby knew he hated reference to personal problems. Any minute now, she might start detailing her mother's ill health. He visibly shivered. 'No problem, no problem. I'll get someone else on it. Make sure you submit your leave form before the end of the day . . .'

Phew. Easier than she'd expected. Seriously, her heart was in overdrive at having to say no to her boss and ask for some holiday. It was pathetic. Her people-pleasing tendencies knew no bounds. Even during her lunch hour, when she finally saw to her grey roots in the hairdresser's next door, she found herself telling the stylist the water temperature was 'just right', when in fact her scalp was being slowly poached.

The hairdresser then proceeded to cut her hair far too short but Libby made sure to leave a large tip and assured her that she loved it. She promptly ran into the ladies' at work and stared at her reflection in the mirror, trying not to cry. 'Perspective,' she said to herself. 'For heaven's sake, get a grip!' She did. She actually focused on her job all afternoon and didn't think about her hair again until she was in the lift at the end of the day and nearly shrieked when she came face to face with her reflection in the overly lit mirrored door. 'Breathe,' she told herself, trying to do that damned mindful breathing again. By the time she reached her car, she was virtually purple in the face.

Breath finally recovered, she drove herself out of the car park and into the thick, unmoving rush hour traffic. *I need to get away*, Libby thought to herself, then remembered that for once she was actually doing just that – getting away. By hurting her wrist, Libby's mum had unwittingly – and at great cost to herself – given her daughter a gift.

Chapter Four

Jersey, November 1941

Queenie's journal

I keep thinking about the last Christmas before the occupation. I can't help it – Mama has started to wonder how we might manage to celebrate this year and it's stirred up my memories. Golly, I sound like an old woman – not a girl of twenty-one.

Back then – Christmas 1939 – I was nineteen and had just started working at Odette's salon, a lovely place run by my friend Sabine's mother. It was an introduction to the world of glamour after five years working on the farm and I was instantly hooked. I'm still working there now, even if Albert thinks I'm too clever for hairstyling. He thinks I should be a teacher, the daft pudding! Even if I were capable, there's not much chance of continuing my education at this point in time and, besides, I can always read now between customers – which is more than I could do when I was working on the farm. I'm devouring *Jane Eyre* again at the moment: my absolute favourite.

But back to Christmas 1939 . . . The war had started then, of course, but nothing much was happening. The 'phoney war' they were calling it and we thought it would all be over within months. Noelle and I were as excited about Christmas as any other year and we set to work on decorating the farmhouse while Mama cooked up a feast and Papa – always smiling then – produced a Christmas tree for us all to dress. The best, though, was when Albert and his family arrived after church on Christmas Day. I answered the door and Mr and Mrs Ecobichon and Kitty and the twins all gave me their coats and hurried through to the warmth of the living room. Happily, Albert held back.

'Shall I take your coat, too?' I smiled.

'Please,' he replied as he blew his dark fringe off his forehead – a little habit I'd taken to daydreaming about. 'Hang on, though, there's something in this pocket,' he said, reaching a hand into the jacket and producing a beautifully wrapped gift.

'Oh, Albert, you shouldn't have! I still haven't got over you giving me a wireless for my eighteenth! I'm still the talk of the village over that. Shall I open it by the fire?'

'No, wait a minute. Open it here,' Albert said. 'Let's just have a moment together.'

It was a bit chilly in the hallway, standing there in my Sunday best (I was wearing the red velvet dress Mama had made me – still my favourite), but I was too happy to care. I ripped open the present and found a copy of Agatha Christie's *The Secret Adversary* – the only one of hers I hadn't read. It smelt delicious, of dusty bookstores – my favourite scent. I flipped open the cover and smiled at the author's dedication to any readers living boring lives in the hope they might experience through the pages of the book some vicarious excitement.

'Oh, Albert, you star! One of my favourite writers . . . You're so clever! Now come through so I can have a proper look at it and I can give you your gift from me. It's not nearly so thoughtful, though, I must admit . . .'

Albert reached out gently to stop me disappearing off. He smiled shyly, producing a small piece of mistletoe from behind his back. I looked around but there was no one else about, so I closed my eyes and stood there, feeling a little bit dizzy and quite foolish. I may even have blushed – not like me at all. But after a few moments I stopped feeling silly because all I knew was that the kiss – our first proper kiss (and about time, too, after two years of courting!) – was the best thing that had ever happened to me. Now, I can't help wondering if it's the best thing that ever will. What a hideously gloomy thought . . .

Christmas. Albert. Both words evoke a sort of magical feeling in my tummy that – for a moment – shifts that newly normal gurgle of hunger. But we must make the best of things, that's what Mama says. Papa has a plan to make sure we eat one of our pigs for Christmas lunch and we're not asking any questions about this. The Germans count all the livestock and so the less we know about the mysterious disappearance of one of the animals, the better.

Though Papa still farms, it's all under the control of the Germans now and it's changed so much: he has to grow wheat instead of potatoes and there are strict controls over the slaughter of livestock. Papa has always grown potatoes – exporting them to England has been his principal income – though he also keeps a dozen dairy cows, a number of pigs and a few chickens, too. It's quite a change for him to have to learn how to grow wheat all of a sudden, though a lot of the farmers are in the same boat, busy reviving the old threshing machines and using a horse and cart just like in years gone by.

Whatever happens, Noelle and I will do our best to drum up a bit of festive spirit – if only for the sake of our parents, though Noelle usually needs a bit of prodding to get into the mood of Christmas. She's got her head in the clouds most of the time, that girl.

At least I'm taking part in the pantomime again this year – a welcome distraction from the humdrum of daily existence. Thank heavens the Germans haven't shut down the dramatic societies, as they have everything else. Papa and I had a good laugh when they closed down the Girl Guides Association, seeing it as some kind of threat. Cynthia

Horsfall, Captain of our local division, *is* quite scary – but hardly a match for Hitler!

In fact, it turns out Miss Horsfall is also rather brave. I'm a Ranger nowadays – far too old to be a Guide – and I just expected we would all obey orders, but Captain has been holding meetings at her house (no uniforms, of course) and we plan to keep the spirit of the movement going, even if we do become limited in how much proper 'Guiding' we can do. I suggested we should start a little library between us so we can lend books to each other and we're coming up with as many inventive needlework ideas as we can. Last week, we spent the meeting making slippers out of old felt hats. Everyone in the family will be getting a pair from me for Christmas! I must admit, it feels exhilarating to be flouting orders from the *Kommandant*, even if it is in quite a small and subtle way. It puts me in mind of a book Miss Horsfall lent me about Van Gogh. Apparently, he once said, '*Great things are done by a series of small things brought together.*' Perhaps that's the very definition of this island's resistance.

Chapter Five

Jersey, December 2016

Liberty

'Can you fit in one last power-walk before you go?' asked Stella. 'I'm on a late tomorrow, so maybe in the morning?'

It was Tuesday and Libby had Stella on speakerphone on her drive home from work.

'I'm going in to the office a bit later than usual tomorrow, so that works. How about eight thirty? Usual place?'

'See you there!' Stella finished, never one for idle chatting on the phone.

The following morning was brisk but another clear and sunny day, one to make the most of, as the forecasters had gloomily predicted rain for the next couple of weeks. Libby was there first and started doing some stretches while she waited for Stella.

'Sorry I'm late!' yelled Stella five minutes later as she stomped towards Libby at the bottom of the cliff steps, Rusty pulling on his lead. 'I overslept! I was going to call you but my phone's dead. I've left it at home to charge. Get down, Rusty! You know, he only jumps up at you. He adores you!'

'I don't mind a bit.'

Within moments they were both panting as they made the steep climb towards the top of the cliff, Rusty leaping ahead and putting them both to shame with his extreme energy levels. In summer, the yellow gorse scented the air with coconut and butterflies fluttered about, making friends with hikers, but in December there was less in the way of insect activity or summery smells. It was no less beautiful, though, and the climbers were rewarded with a stunning view of L'Etacq when they reached the top. Aside from the number of cars trundling along on the network of lanes below them, the view couldn't have changed much in centuries. The magnificent sandy bay, the sea a kaleidoscope of greens and blues, the other islands in the distance, the fields and farm buildings, the moss-covered granite walls, dark rocks and shadowy cliffs. It was timeless and had the effect it always had on Libby, immediately starting to calm her.

'Have you packed yet?' asked Stella as they began to make their way along the cliff path.

'No, I've been trying to get the house sorted and everything organised for Henry and Milo before I start on me.'

'You shouldn't do it, you know. You do far more than your fair share in your household, Libby.'

'I know, and it's my own fault. I should make a stand more with Henry and the children. But you know what I'm like.'

'I know. Anything for a quiet life,' sighed Stella, resigned to her friend's hopelessness. 'Anyway, it's Wednesday, so that must mean Henry's cooking tonight!'

'Exactly!' Libby replied, smiling. 'Hang on,' she said as her phone began to ring. She felt her head start to spin as she listened to the person on the other end. 'Stella . . .' she said, handing the phone towards her friend. 'It's Ben.'

'Ben, my ex-husband Ben?' asked Stella, laughing. 'What the hell's he doing calling you?'

'He couldn't get hold of you on your phone. He was still on the list as one of your mum's next of kin. Ben will explain. I'm so sorry, Stella . . .'

Stella's smile vanished as she took the phone. Libby waited, the wind whipping around her ears.

'What is it? What's happened? Ben only said that your mum's not well . . .' Libby asked when Stella passed her friend the phone and stood there on the cliffs, looking shattered.

'She's . . . erm, she's had another stroke,' Stella said, her voice faltering. 'They . . . They don't think she's going to make it. I've got to get there. To the hospital. Now.'

'Of course. Come on – I'll drive you there. You're not in a fit state.'

They stumbled to the bottom of the cliff, then drove in silence. When they reached the hospital, Libby turned off the engine and turned to Stella. 'I'll just park up and then I'll come and find you.'

'No. No, Libs. You go to work. It's kind of you but, you know . . . My mum . . .'

Stella didn't need to finish the sentence. Sybil had never liked Libby, though Libby had never managed to work out why. The last thing Sybil would want would be to see Libby at her side at a time like this.

'Of course,' Libby said, squeezing her friend's hand. 'But if you need me, just call. I can always wait in the corridor. You're going to need someone.'

'I know. I will need you. When it happens. I'll ring you.'

Libby felt horribly distracted, thinking about her friend all day, but in the afternoon she received a call to say Sybil was stable and, reassured that Stella was coping, she vowed to concentrate on her own family for the evening.

Wednesday was Milo's drumming lesson, involving a fifteen-minute drive each way and a half-an-hour wait in the car. Libby's friends from the mainland always remarked on how Jersey was so small that surely it was no effort whatsoever to get about, laughing if she used the word 'commute'. But the truth was that the island was crawling with cars – most of them posh and miles too big for the tiny roads – and at peak times the traffic could be hideous. But this particular journey was actually one of the highlights of the week for Libby. There were few cars on the roads by seven o'clock, so the journey was smooth, and now that Milo didn't like to talk to her she could listen to *The Archers* on Radio 4: one of the few daily events that calmed and soothed her. Milo complained as soon as the jaunty theme tune began but he soon put in his earphones and shrank into his collar, looking balefully out of the window while Libby sighed and sat back to enjoy the show.

Her absence between seven and eight on a Wednesday also meant that, for one night of the week, supper had to be organised by Henry. Admittedly, Libby still went through the boring process of deciding what they should eat and buying the ingredients, but she always looked forward to returning home to find the lights in the kitchen aglow and a scent of frying onions and garlic filling the air.

Tonight was no exception and, as Henry greeted her at the back door with a kiss, she felt a pang as she realised she'd miss her family during her trip away – though she was soon revising that opinion after Henry burned the onions and Amy turned up at the front door unannounced, full of venom at having learned through Liam that Libby was going away for a week.

'I can't believe how selfish you're being,' she complained before she'd even shrugged off her coat. She handed it to Libby as though her mother were a maid. Libby rolled her eyes and hung it up in the downstairs cloakroom. 'Mum, the wedding's only three months away and you know I'm meant to be seeing the venue and the caterers next week! I can't believe you're vanishing off to Canterbury and leaving me to deal with it all. I've got an extremely stressful job, you know! Bethany wouldn't have to deal with this. Her mother's involved in every little detail of her wedding. She's virtually doing it all for her!'

Libby tried to bite down her anger at the injustice of this outburst. She pulled a bottle of wine out of the fridge and, after checking it was superior enough for Amy's standards, uncorked it. 'But you didn't want me to interfere! You expressly told me when you got engaged that you wanted to be in charge of it all, with Dad and I just stumping up the cash.'

'Oh, here we go, making me feel guilty about the money. I've budgeted as much as I can, you know, but it's not easy trying to do a wedding on the cheap!'

Libby gasped at this. 'On the cheap? It's costing nigh on ten thousand pounds. We could almost put a deposit down on a house of our own for that, couldn't we, Henry?' Libby's attempt to haul Henry into the conversation was in vain, though, as he was a terrible ostrich; he just turned up the extractor fan above the oven to drown out the bickering. Libby closed her eyes and took a breath.

'Amy, darling, let's not argue. I'm sorry I forgot to tell you but there's a lot to organise. And I'm not doing it to spite anybody. Granny's had a fall and sprained her wrist. They need a helping hand. And I miss them. I haven't seen them in ages.'

'Well, why can't they just come here?' asked Amy a little more quietly, though her mouth was still petulant. She'd had that petulant lip since she was about a year old.

Henry did turn round at this.

'I hadn't thought of that. Doesn't that make more sense?' he asked.

'They won't leave the cats, even in that smart cattery down the road. The last time they did, when they went on that cruise, they missed them too much,' Libby explained. 'And anyway, you're all perfectly capable of getting on with life without me for a week. Perhaps it will be a good thing. Maybe you'll miss me,' she said, gulping down some wine like her life depended on it. She felt a sudden urge to abandon her family and call Stella, but then remembered that her friend had far worse troubles of her own.

'Of course we will,' Henry told her as he began to serve up their meal.

Milo grunted at this and Amy just harrumphed. 'Well, please at least make sure you keep your phone on. I'll need to give you a call every day about the wedding.'

'I will,' Libby agreed, taking the peace offering, such as it was. 'Now tell me, how's the groom?'

'The groom?' Amy asked.

'You know . . . Jonty . . .'

'Oh, he's fine. He's always fine,' she said, dismissing him instantly, and Libby had to smile to herself. The poor man had been completely forgotten by the bride in her manic desire to create the perfect wedding. How it had all changed since she and Henry had married. Nowadays, as a heavily filtered load of pictures would no doubt be posted on Facebook within twenty-four hours of the wedding taking place, a decent photographer seemed to be the highest priority.

Libby was just clearing away the detritus of the meal while Amy flicked through a magazine at the table, Henry having disappeared to his study and Milo to his room, when her phone began to ring. It was Stella.

'Stella. What's happened?'

The silence at the other end was followed by a sob. 'She's bloody died, Libby. I didn't think it was going to happen this soon. She was so lucid for a short time this afternoon. I just can't believe it. I can't believe she's gone.'

'Oh, Stella. I'm so, so sorry. Where are you now?'

'I've just got home.'

'I'll be there. Sit tight. I'll be there in five.'

Chapter Six

Yesterday was quite a day. It started off well enough – Sabine and I decided to make a trip into town to see a film on at the Forum as it's early closing at the salon on a Tuesday. We didn't want to see any of the German films they put on there but we'd heard they had *It Happened One Night* on and, although we'd seen it before, it was an outing at least. When Noelle heard about our plan, she asked if she could come with her friends Rachel and Sybil, too.

I hesitated. I wasn't worried about Rachel but Sybil was another matter. 'Oh, go on then,' I agreed in the end. 'But tell Sybil she's not to get us into trouble this time.' Sybil's a lovely girl – a real character. She's decided since war broke out to dress like a British factory girl, even though she doesn't have a job in one, so every time I see her she's sporting a boiler suit and has her strawberry blonde hair tied up in one of those headscarves like a turban. She's very amusing, and loyal as anything, but she can be a bit feisty, especially around the Germans. Last time we went to the pictures with her, she started jeering at the propaganda before the film and we were chucked out.

Noelle couldn't get hold of Rachel but Sybil came along and this time she was good as gold for the whole performance, so I was feeling nice and relaxed as we left the Forum. We were wandering along towards the bus stop, Noelle and Sabine a little way ahead and me and Sybil following behind, remarking on how hungry the poor town folk looked, when, as we turned the corner, a rowdy group of drunken *Luftwaffe* officers came lumbering along four abreast, knocking Noelle clean off the pavement. I immediately hopped off the path to make way for them but Sybil stood steadfast right in the middle of it, clearly infuriated by their treatment of her friend. When they reached her they stopped, taken aback by the stand Sybil had decided to take.

'Don't fancy knocking me sideways off the pavement, too, then?' she asked, sarcastic like she often is. The sarcasm was lost on the Germans.

'Step to one side, so we may pass,' one of them said, his voice cheerful. His colleagues sniggered.

'Oh, you're all attached? I didn't realise the four of you were sewn together! That's why you can't make way for a lady! It must make life very difficult.'

'Vot is your name?' the man asked, sounding much cooler.

'Vot's it to you?' Sybil asked, and I felt my legs turn to jelly. Sybil gets the devil in her sometimes.

'I vill ask you one more time,' said the officer. 'Either you move or you vill be spending the next veek in prison.'

You could see it pained her to do so, but she stepped off the pavement and the four officers carried on towards the Forum, loud and brash and victorious. Sybil wasn't going to let them have the last word though.

'Pigs!' she shouted back, and then we all ran off, fast as we could, towards the bus stop. Fortunately, the officers couldn't be bothered to chase us.

Mightily relieved that Sybil hadn't got us all into serious trouble, we took the bus back home in good time before curfew and said our goodbyes in the village, before Noelle and I walked down the hill to L'Etacq. As ever nowadays, we went to bed soon after we'd eaten supper.

For some reason, though, I was struggling to sleep, so I started reading while everyone else in the farmhouse slept – by candlelight, as we're not allowed to use electricity between eleven at night and seven in the morning. The grandfather clock downstairs struck twelve and the wind was howling, the windows rattling in their frames, when I realised I could hear another noise, too. A low, distinct groaning. An animal? I went to the window and pulled up the blackout blind so I could open the sash and I heard it again. A horrible noise – the kind I'd defy anyone with a heart to ignore. I pulled on my thick dressing gown and slippers and took the candle with me down the creaky wooden stairs and through to the kitchen, where I unlocked the back door. Out there, the noise was louder. It was coming from just up along the lane. My candle blew out but the moon was full and so I crept along and just hoped to goodness there'd be no German soldiers passing by on patrol.

I came across the source of the groaning only about fifty yards along the lane. A man, thin as a rake and with a shaved head, was curled up in a ball in the middle of the road! I could smell him even from a couple of feet away.

'Are you hurt?' I asked. The man's head shot up and he looked at me with large, beseeching eyes. He stopped groaning and immediately a torrent of some foreign language poured from his mouth. Russian? Papa sometimes used to speak like that to Mamie, who was half Russian. The lad only seemed to know one English word: 'please'. There was no doubt he was in dire need.

'Follow me,' I whispered. 'Can you walk?' The waif pulled himself up from the lane with great effort and hobbled after me. I took him into the kitchen and sat him in the armchair by the stove, then I went upstairs to wake Papa and Mama.

'Papa,' I whispered urgently. 'Papa, there was a man in the lane. I heard groaning so I went outside and found this poor wretch – he's in the kitchen now . . . Papa, he looks so thin and he stinks to high heaven! I think he's one of the Russian slave workers,' I gabbled.

'Good Lord,' Papa grumbled, rubbing his eyes. 'What are you doing going out after curfew, Queenie? And you can't bring Russian workers into the house! We'll all end up in prison!' But despite his grumbling, Papa was a welcoming host to his unexpected guest, as was Mama, who came downstairs wrapped in her dressing gown and with her clogs on. She immediately tended to the man's raw and bleeding feet. She isn't squeamish – she was a midwife until her varicose veins got the better of her. After a quiet word with Mama, Papa made bramble-leaf tea and I found the Russian a hunk of bread and some of our homemade jam while casting surreptitious looks at him. I could see that in another life – one in which he hadn't been starved or suffered the atrocities that had given him a face shadowed by fear – he would have been exceptionally attractive.

'Mama,' I whispered as she disposed of the rags she'd used to tend to the stranger's feet in the wash house annexed to the kitchen. 'He was groaning so badly. Is he ill?'

'Only a doctor could tell us that but – aside from his poor feet – there's nothing obviously wrong. I think he was beside himself with hunger and exhaustion.'

'Why was he there, out on the lane?'

'Well, I can't understand him any more than you can, my love, but I imagine he was trying to run away from that camp up the road. Those poor men are living in utter squalor and then they're expected to do a full day's slave labour working on those ugly fortifications. I expect he'd reached his limit. Physically and mentally.'

'What will we do? Can we keep him here?'

'No, it's not safe. Too much coming and going with the four of us here. But Papa has an idea. You mustn't ask about it, though. You head off to bed, my precious. The less you know, the better.' I kissed Mama and headed out through the kitchen towards the stairs, looking back at Papa, who was rubbing the man's back, speaking gently in his language.

'And Queenie . . .' Mama called out, following me. I turned around. 'Well done, my love. You did the right thing. We mustn't let this situation we're in turn us into rotten apples. It was right – to help him.'

I smiled and returned to bed but I couldn't sleep, so I lay there listening to the distant sound of gunfire in France and wondering what Papa was going to do to help this man. Oleg, he's called. Knowing his name . . . it changes things. So far, the *Wehrmacht* soldiers I've come across haven't been so bad – certainly not what we were expecting. With the exception of the *Gestapo*, whom I've only heard rumours of so far, and the arrogant *Luftwaffe* officers, they seem polite: scholarly, even. Not exactly the savage beasts we feared when the island became occupied. The ordinary soldiers (Papa calls them 'greenflies' due to their green uniforms) give sweets to the kids and seem on the whole to be just normal family men missing their own children.

But every so often you hear of something really nasty happening, like that poor Frenchman being shot in the grounds of St Ouen's Manor, and now – seeing the state of the Russian slave worker – it really brings home just how terrible a situation we're all in. And I'm caught between the fear of Papa not helping Oleg and the horror of knowing that if, as Mama promises, he does help him, and he's caught, then Papa will be punished. Severely. And, no matter which way I look at it, it will all be my fault.

Chapter Seven

Jersey, December 2016

Liberty

Libby arrived at Stella's cottage and, not bothering to ring the bell, pushed open the stable door. She found Stella standing by the Rayburn, staring into space.

'You didn't hear what I said, then,' Stella said, sounding weird.

'You said you'd just got home,' Libby replied, dumping her handbag, about to encompass her friend in a hug. But something stopped her. Stella's pain was so raw Libby wasn't sure if she'd be receptive to being touched.

'I also said don't come round but you must have put the phone down.'

'Oh, I'm sorry! Is it too soon? I understand,' Libby said, picking up her bag again. 'I know it's not the same but when Granny Noelle died just after Amy was born, I didn't want to see anyone for a day or two either, do you remember?'

'Don't mention that name in this house!' Stella spat out, and Libby realised her friend wasn't just sad. She was angry. Furious.

'Granny Noelle? But why not?'

'Don't play the innocent with me, Liberty.' Libby quaked at the formal use of her name. 'Don't tell me you didn't know all these years what your grandparents did to my mother and her parents!'

'Stella, I've got no idea what you're talking about! I know Sybil didn't get on with them and she was always funny with Mum and Dad and me but, Stella, neither of us knew why, did we? We always used to say it was odd!'

'Then maybe it's high time you found out!'

'Found out what?'

'You ask your father about the grudge, see if he'll tell you the truth! But you'd better get out of here right now, Liberty, because I can't stand the sight of you!'

Stella was terrifying. Libby had seen her like this before with other people who had crossed her, as well as in defence of Libby on numerous occasions, but they'd never fallen out before. This cold fury had never once been directed at Libby.

Libby retreated to the door and stumbled out of it, forgetting the step that caught most visitors out, though Libby had never tripped on it before. She threw herself into the Volvo and drove home, only bursting into tears when she reached the Vicarage. What on earth was Stella on about? What could be so utterly terrible that she couldn't even bear to look at Libby? She recalled Stella saying that Sybil had been lucid for a short period in the afternoon. Had Sybil, on her deathbed, told her daughter some tale of old about Granny Noelle and Grandpa John that for some reason now destroyed their friendship? There was only one way she was going to find out. She would have to ask her father. Libby contemplated calling him but Alf was no good on the phone. She would bide her time until she arrived in Canterbury and would find a moment then to ask him what could possibly have been so catastrophic.

42

'Now, you're not to worry about Stella. She'll come round. Talk to your dad and see what he says. You know, I'm really going to miss you,' Henry told Libby as they said their goodbyes next to the check-in desk two days later. He tucked her hair behind her ears – something he'd done all the time when they were first together. Libby couldn't remember the last time he'd made that gesture.

'I'll miss you, too,' she said, hugging him intently. 'But it's only a week.'

'Make sure you rest, won't you? As well as looking after your mum. You need it,' Henry said, touching the dark circles under Libby's eyes. She found herself immediately irritated. She didn't need reminding about those.

Oblivious to the fact that his parting comment had annoyed her, Henry was off a moment later, waving cheerily. Libby was about to head through to Departures when she saw Liam dashing across the check-in area towards her, almost knocking the Christmas tree flying, his hair dishevelled and with fair stubble on his chin. His work shirt was hanging out over his suit trousers and, as he got closer, she could see his eyes were bloodshot.

'Mum!' he shouted. 'Mum, please don't go! I need you here. Mum, I can't bear it if you go,' he pleaded. Libby felt his words pull at her heartstrings but she'd heard it all a million times before.

The terrible plea from an eleven-year-old Liam – 'Mummy, I don't want to go on the French trip. Don't make me go! I'll hate every minute. Don't do this to me!' – had been followed by a dreadful, guilt-ridden few days for Libby, who'd insisted that he go, positive he'd enjoy it once he got there.

'He had the time of his life,' Liam's form teacher later informed her when Libby arrived, with bitten-down nails, to pick Liam up from the ferry. She'd expected him to dash into her arms but instead she found him laughing and joshing with his schoolmates, in no rush to embrace his mother after all.

'Liam, you've had a heavy night by the looks of things,' she told him now. 'You're just feeling vulnerable, my darling. Go back to your flat and have a bath, then get work out of the way and have a nice early night.' Hard as it was, Libby hugged Liam briefly and swiftly left him behind, making her way towards Security. A quick goodbye was always best with Liam.

Five minutes later she received a text. *Seriously, Mum, I need you! Please come back!* With superhuman effort, Libby turned off her phone – a supremely rare occurrence but one that was sometimes necessary when Liam became a little too ready with the guilt-inducing text messages – and made her way to the cafe. She bought herself a cup of tea and used about seven little pots of UHT milk to get herself a reasonable-looking brew.

It had always been this way with Liam. It was the main reason Libby had so rarely left her family over the years. But she'd learned from experience that, heart-rending though it was, to kowtow to Liam was actually to do him a disservice.

She was buying the latest *Hello!* magazine in the airport newsagent's when her heart suddenly jumped to attention. Just ahead of her in the queue was Stella, dressed in one of her hippy skirts and a multicoloured cheesecloth top. What was she doing going away when her mum had just died? It must be something important to do with her job. Libby observed her friend's familiar gestures. The way she tossed back her mass of strawberry blonde hair; her impatient hopping from one foot to the other. Libby was frozen with indecision. Should she tap Stella on the shoulder? Wait to see if she spotted her? Before she'd made up her mind, Stella had paid for her newspaper and turned around. Libby saw the brief flash of panic on her friend's face.

'Libby! Fancy seeing you here! Are you off somewhere nice?' she asked in a weird voice. The stilted and superficial question stabbed at Libby's heart. The fact that Stella was feigning politeness was somehow worse than if she'd just snubbed Libby altogether.

'I'm off to Canterbury to see Mum and Dad, remember? How about you? Work or pleasure?' Oh, heavens, she was even worse than Stella. She sounded like a travel agent.

'Work, as usual. Conference on "legal highs" in Holborn. I should be able to get the last flight home. How long are you away again?'

Libby had by now reached the front of the queue and Stella seized the chance to escape, not waiting for Libby's answer. 'I'll leave you to it,' Stella said, and she was off, before Libby even had a chance to ask how she was coping and when the funeral was likely to be. As they were on the same flight, Libby had to spend the next couple of hours trying to avoid further awkward conversations in the various gathering points: the lounge, the departure gate, the plane, the baggage hall, even the train station at Gatwick. By the time she reached Canterbury, Libby was ecstatic to be free of the small-community burden of bumping into friends and enemies or, in her case, both her best friend and, it now seemed, her worst enemy.

The train pulled into Canterbury West. She heaved her case onto the platform and looked around. She heard a voice call 'Libby!' and she was soon in the steadying arms of her father, Alf. He was never effusive, but she could tell he was happy to see her. He couldn't hide the joy in his kindly blue eyes. He looked just the same as always: tall, handsome and almost completely bald now, though once he'd boasted a head of fine blond curls. His eyebrows remained blond and bushy, making him look endearingly like a mad professor.

'Best get you home,' he mumbled. 'Mum's killed the fatted calf!' Alf then took Libby's case for her and guided her out of the station towards his waiting truck. He'd inherited the truck from his mother, Noelle. It had survived the German wartime occupation of Jersey – which was quite remarkable, as most of the islanders' vehicles had been requisitioned by the Germans – and was her father's most precious possession. It was a little draughty and clunky now – unsurprisingly, as it dated from the 1930s – but immaculately kept.

They arrived at the cul-de-sac in Mead Way after a short drive and, as Libby saw her parents' terraced house hove into view, she knew she'd find their home similarly immaculate and no doubt festooned with Christmas decorations. Her mother – known to everyone as 'Tink' – was absolutely crackers about the festive season, an obsession that had rubbed off on Libby. She'd always been madly excited about Christmas – until this year. Somehow her state of mind hadn't yet granted her the necessary mental space for all the usual buying, wrapping, card writing, decorating and organising . . . She'd still need to do all that nearer to Christmas but for now – for a week at least – the pressure was off.

'In we go, then,' said Alf. Libby opened the front door to the tiny lobby and went straight through to the living room. A doorway led through to the kitchen – a square room with peach-coloured cabinets – and Libby's mother appeared in it, adorned, as ever, in a floral apron.

'Darling girl!' she beamed, stretching up on tiptoes to kiss Libby, then snuggling into her for a cuddle like a little child. She was barely five feet tall, with dainty bones, and her hair, once strikingly long and dark, was now a fluffy, white crop like a dandelion clock.

'Hi, Mum,' Libby replied. 'How's your wrist?'

'Oh, it's fine. I can do nearly everything despite the splint. You didn't need to come, though I'm glad you did.'

They took a step back and looked at each other, grinning. They had a simple relationship –always happy to be in each other's company, laughing at daft things. Tink had a wonderful sense of the ridiculous and was a supreme chatterbox, two characteristics that made her hugely warm and popular. She was a joy to be around. Libby observed her father looking on at their reunion fondly. Dear Alf was a different cup of tea – a quieter, more serious soul, but steady and wise; always full of the best advice. Not that he'd push it on you; he had a knack for knowing when you might be receptive to it.

'Like a cuppa?' asked Tink.

'I could murder one,' Libby replied.

'Kettle's just boiled. Come and chat to me while I make it, then we'll bring it through. I've done your favourite rainbow-coloured sandwiches and I've got those marshmallow biscuit things you like.'

Libby smiled to herself. Though nicknamed Tink, her mother was actually like Peter Pan, and she seemed to think everyone else was, too. But Libby was more than happy to be treated like a child. Perhaps it was just what she needed.

Before long, the three of them were sitting with their knees under the dining table at one end of the living room, enjoying Tink's version of afternoon tea and listening to her chitter-chatter while Coco and Chanel – the Persian cats – sat regally on the piano, watching the humans with disdain, though they wouldn't say no to a morsel of smoked salmon.

'Elsie from next door had a terrible fall last night. We heard her, didn't we, Alf? Your father went round and saved the day. Called 999, though they're terribly slow these days. Overburdened and underpaid, I expect. Over an hour the dear old duck had to wait with a broken hip! Poor thing had only just returned from her cruise the day before. Talking of which, did I ever tell you about those funny people we met on that cruise we went on for my seventieth?'

'No, I don't think so,' Libby replied.

'Man and wife, in their forties – maybe even fifties – and every night they appeared somewhere or other on the ship, each clutching a teddy bear!' Tink recounted, her eyes wide with amusement.

'No! But why? Maybe they were simple?'

'Nothing wrong with them! I chatted to them a lot and they were perfectly normal, if you can believe it. Just exhibitionists, I think – they certainly received a lot of attention. Honestly, I'd be stood there speaking to the chap and suddenly he'd start doing a ventriloquist-type thing, making his teddy bear do the talking!'

Amused by the recollection, Tink's eyes filled with tears of laughter. It never took much to send her over the edge. Her mirth was so contagious Libby couldn't help needing to reach for a tissue herself to dab her eyes. It was marvellously therapeutic. Alf looked on, quietly bemused.

'Were they the same teddies? Did the man and his wife have matching ones?' asked Libby, through her giggles.

'No! The wife had a panda; don't ask me why!'

'Did the panda like to chat, too?'

Tink had by now just about managed to compose herself, but this question set her off again, her shoulders shaking with mirth as she reached for another tissue. 'You tell her!' she just about managed to say to Alf.

'The panda didn't do much talking, no,' Alf said. 'The panda preferred to dance.'

'Oh, don't!' Libby giggled. 'Who with? The other teddy?' But by now it was hopeless trying to get sense out of either of her parents, as Alf had finally succumbed and was chortling away. It took the shrill announcement of the doorbell to calm them all down.

'Oh, heavens, that'll be my physio!' exclaimed Tink. 'Look at the state of me.' She hopped up and dabbed at her red cheeks with another tissue, then quickly took off her apron. 'Do I look presentable?' she asked.

'Absolutely,' Libby told her. 'I'll clear the tea up while you're having your treatment,' she said, starting to stack the crockery and shoving it through the hatch from the dining area into the kitchen. Alf helped, drying the dishes as Libby washed, then plodded through to the living room to conduct his jobs: winding the carriage clock on the mantelpiece and laying the fire for the evening. While Alf busied himself, Libby decided to reacquaint herself with the house, inspecting each of the little rooms and listening with pleasure to the regular rattle of the trains passing on the railway line behind the garden fence.

It was rather nice being able to look around the house at her leisure, relishing the familiarity of it all. She'd lived there from the age of fifteen until she'd left for university, shortly after which she'd married Henry, who, though they'd met in London, had turned out, by some incredible coincidence, to be a Jersey-man. He and Libby had never once met in Jersey – Henry had gone to school in the east of the island – but after studying in London, he'd taken a job as the vicar of St George's in Millais (just up the hill from L'Etacq, in the parish of St Ouen), meaning that Libby had been able to return to her childhood home, only a short distance from the beloved farmhouse she'd grown up in.

The tour didn't take long. Downstairs, there was a lean-to attached to the kitchen, which led out to the garden and vegetable patch; then, on the other side of the kitchen was the dining area and the living room with fireplace, threadbare sofa and wing armchairs, as well as windows looking onto the street outside.

Through the lobby and up the stairs there were three bedrooms and a single bathroom. Tink was in the main bedroom receiving her treatment, so Libby made her way along the narrow landing to the guest rooms. One was tiny – a box room really, with just enough space for the single bed, neatly covered with a floral counterpane, and a small desk, which was where Tink wrote her novels, though currently she'd had a break imposed on her by her bad wrist. Tink had never managed to find a publisher but was quite happy to self-publish. The financial rewards weren't much to write home about but it was clear the satisfaction Tink achieved from writing far outweighed anything else. The books were rather racy ones, apparently, and as a result Libby hadn't quite brought herself around to reading them. But Stella said they were some of the best of that genre.

The other room was where Libby would be staying and where Alf had kindly deposited her suitcase like a porter. Tink had been hard at work, despite her bad wrist, and the room was gleaming clean, its two single beds made up with freshly laundered sheets and blankets, with pink bedspreads pulled back. A large mahogany wardrobe took up half the room, but it was one of the many pieces of furniture her parents hadn't wanted to part with when they'd moved house.

It was all just heart-warmingly homely. But what was really comforting was the way Tink had introduced Christmas into every corner of the house. On each and every windowsill were lovely little lights that imitated lit candles, making the place feel cosy and welcoming. There were touchingly childish paper chains hanging from the ceiling in every room, the scent of M&S festive potpourri tickled Libby's nostrils everywhere she went and back downstairs, the tree – far too big for the living room – smelt of pine needles and was groaning with decorations and great swathes of gold and silver tinsel, which Libby always found a bit gaudy but Tink adored.

'Dad!' Libby called, finding the living room empty, then she spotted him through the window, out in the garden, filling the ceramic bird-bath with fresh water. She was about to join him when her phone rang.

'Amy, darling!' she answered, and, as she listened to the torrent begin, she felt her heart rate, which had calmed as she arrived in Canterbury, increase to its normal unhealthy level. 'Slow down!' she ordered her daughter. 'I can't understand a word you're saying.'

'Mum, it's the caterers. They've gone bust! They won't honour our booking! We're going to have to find another company, but it's far too late in the day! We'll never find anything – it's only twelve weeks now . . . And you've gone off on this stupid jaunt of yours and I'm here trying to sort this mess out on my own! Oh my goodness! I can't even breathe!'

'Calm down, Amy. It'll all be fine. Nobody gets married in March. I'm sure we'll be able to find someone.'

'But I just haven't got the time to ring round! I'm working on this case! It's a nightmare! I'm having to pull all-nighters . . .'

Libby closed her eyes, accepting the inevitable. 'Leave it with me,' she said. 'I'll get it sorted, I promise.'

'Will you?' Amy asked, sounding quite normal again. 'Oh, Mum, you are wonderful. Thank you so much. Will you call me once you've found someone?'

'Of course. Amy, you will look in on Dad and Milo for me, won't you? And Liam. He seemed a bit vulnerable this morning.'

'Oh yes, sure, will do . . . Mum, I've got to go. I've got an important call coming in. Speak soon.'

'Okay, sweetheart. Bye. Love you.'

But Amy was gone.

Chapter Eight

Jersey, November 1941

Queenie's journal

A lot to write about today! It's been more than a week since the incident with Oleg and, up to this morning, I'd no idea whether Papa was helping him. I kept wondering what Papa could possibly do. As far as I could tell, he wasn't hiding him in the farmhouse. I had a good hunt around the farm yesterday – my day off – and searched high and low in the barn and the hayloft and the soot house, but there wasn't any sign of Oleg. I kept thinking about him and his deep-set eyes – haunted, yet striking: the greeny blue of the shallows in St Ouen's Bay on a sunny day.

Then this morning I was distracted from thinking about the Russian by some gossip at the salon. I love working at Odette's. I always thought I'd be working on the farm, at least until I married, but when my friend Sabine's mother, Odette, asked if I'd be interested in an apprenticeship, I was chuffed to bits. I love having a uniform – I feel a bit like a nurse in it! – and I haven't looked back, even if Albert thinks I should be a teacher instead! It's ever such hard work, but an absolute lark as well.

It's also the source of much gossip, which comes in extremely handy at the moment, when communication is so difficult.

Sabine and I have been friends since we were tiny and the single fly in the ointment of our friendship has only ever been a girl called Mary Jane. She's the kind of friend who's always engaged in mind games, try-ing to play one friend off against the other. For years, this caused a lot of strife between Sabine and me until – having talked things through together – we realised we were like two little mice being batted around by a mischievous cat. After that, Mary Jane lost some of her power but she didn't seem to want to make many other friends, so she's always tried to remain close to the two of us.

But since the occupation started, we haven't seen hide nor hair of Mary Jane. Sabine and I have been speculating wildly on what she might have been up to – had she escaped to England on a boat? Was she unwell? We asked our friends but nobody seemed to know where she was or what she was doing. She'd been working at a butcher's in the market until about a year ago, when she'd been 'let go', joining the increasing number of unemployed, and there'd been no sign of her since. This was something of a relief to me, I admit, although I was also a little concerned that she seemed to have vanished into thin air. I do see Mary Jane's mother from time to time, as she works as a cleaner up at one of the village schools. A lovely woman, she is – salt of the earth. But I don't like to ask her what's happened to Mary Jane in case it isn't good news and it upsets her.

Anyway . . . the gossip! I was trimming old Tommy Le Brun's hair this morning: he's the village butcher and has a mass of wild white hair that often needs taming. He always tucks his trousers into his socks when he cycles about and never sees the point in pulling them out again, or maybe he just forgets. As I started to chop away at his mad hair, he began grumbling about the 'Jerrybags'. We've all heard about these women – the locals who are favoured by the Germans and unscrupulously lord it about the place, wearing furs and jewels stolen from the houses left vacant by islanders who fled the island before the occupation, most of which have now been requisitioned by the high-ranking officers.

'Those girls, flirting with the Jerries and drinking the cellars of those lovely houses dry . . . They ought to know better, eh . . . Little floozies,' Tommy was muttering. He has very few teeth, so it was quite hard to understand the rest of his complaint, but I got the general idea – in essence, he was livid about the Jerrybags and even more livid about the dastardly Jerries. Tommy has a terrible temper on him, which we all fear will get him into trouble.

Tommy is a true Jersey bean and, like the rest of us, he's fluent in the island's native tongue, Jèrriais. He's also known for his intense hatred of the Germans. He speaks in patois as often as possible – usually making insulting comments – knowing the Jerries won't understand him. Anyone in earshot who's local has to be careful not to laugh.

But back to the story in hand . . . So then I heard a name I recog-nised – Mary Jane.

'Did you say Mary Jane?' I asked, pausing in my snipping to look Tommy in the eye through the mirror opposite us. I chose the one on the left as his eyes look in different directions.

'Mary Jane . . . You know – that scrawny girl with the *couleu d'vaque* hair – yellow brown, like a cow; 'bout your age she is. One of the senior ones has taken a fancy to her; he's called Kurt von Grimmelshausen, but he's known as 'the Grim One' – he's a nasty bit of work, eh. He's part of that civil affairs unit – the *Feldkommandantur*, or whatever stupid name it has! A civil servant dressed up in uniform!'

'What does he look like?' I asked, wondering if I might have come across him.

'You know the expression "*aver eune minne dé cat rôti*"?'

I looked blank, which riled Tommy.

'*Sacrébleu!* Nobody can speak their own bloody language these days! You ask your father – he'll tell you it means to look like death warmed up! Pale as a corpse, that Nazi is. Distinctive, as well, eh – long scar across his face. The rotter took my butcher's van off me when they started doing all that blasted requisitioning. Daylight robbery! Anyway, saw her yesterday, I did, that Mary Jane. I was queuing for eggs and some enormous black car pulled up. Mary Jane gets out, looking all posh and la-di-da and just swaggers to the front of the queue, asks for all the eggs available – leaving the rest of us with sod all – and swans back to the car. She only had a bleeding chauffeur! She'll get her come-uppance, that girl – you mark my words.'

I was itching to tell Sabine, but she was busy trying to make Phyllis Bisson look like Betty Grable, so she had her work cut out. Fortunately, Sabine was coming to the farmhouse to stay overnight, so we said our goodbyes to Odette at four o'clock and cycled down the hill towards home in the gloaming. Freewheeling down Mont Pinel with a view of the tumbling waves in the distance, I could almost forget there was a war on, though if we'd ventured nearer to the beach, the barbed wire surrounding our beautiful bay would have been an instant reminder.

I think that's what I miss the most – being able to walk for miles along the golden sands. One of my favourite games as a young girl was to run from the slipway next to the farmhouse all the way along the beach to the one at La Saline, racing an incoming tide. It was silly of me, looking back, but I've not known anything as exhilarating since. But you wouldn't risk going to the beach now, whether you were racing the tide or not: Papa says it's full of mines. Mind you, while they can stop us going on the beaches, they can't prevent us from enjoying the sounds and sights of the sea. My favourite tide is a ferociously high one at bedtime. I love listening to the boomers pounding at night. It's hard to tell sometimes what's the sound of the ocean and what's the noise of bombing and gunfire coming from across the water or the skies above us when our British fighter pilots come too close.

I filled Sabine in on the Mary Jane scandal as we cycled together along the lane that leads to the farmhouse. (Papa joked the other day that, before we know it, the Germans will ban us from cycling two abreast! Every day, there seems to be another rule to obey and some of them are so silly.)

'No!' Sabine gasped at the news, her dark eyebrows raised and her slanting hazelnut eyes wide. 'No wonder she's gone underground. Wouldn't want to come across us, would she, or any of her old friends? She'd get a mouthful, all right, and well deserved. Well, that explains it, anyway. We had her escaping the island or under the weather but we didn't think she'd be fraternising with the enemy, did we?'

'Apparently, she's hooked up with one of the senior ones,' I went on. 'The Grim One, he's called. She's even got a chauffeur! And she was all dolled up, so Tommy said. She always was a one for glamour.'

'Well, we're all missing a bit of glamour in our lives these days but that's no reason to go walking out with a German, is it?'

Sabine spoke with no small passion, for until recently she'd attended the weekly dances at the Plaza – where Albert and I used to dance before the war (I've such fond memories of our dances to Bing Crosby's 'Stardust'). Some of the Germans go dancing with local girls there now and a senior officer took a shine to Sabine, beguiled by her sultry beauty. There's a wholesome, fresh look about my friend, with her clear skin and her shining pageboy haircut. She's always been a head-turner.

Anyway, this officer started bringing her little gifts – delicately scented soaps from Paris and silky smooth nylons – but Sabine refused them. It must have taken great resolve: any old soap is scarce these days, but those Parisian ones must have been a temptation like no other. And when Odette found out about it all, she banned Sabine from going to the dances any longer. Noelle and I comforted her about this loss of entertainment as best we could, having never been allowed to attend ourselves, much to our annoyance: Papa won't countenance us dancing with any Germans. He fought in the last war and can't bear to see the enemy swanning about his homeland.

By the time we arrived at the farmhouse, it was dark. As we entered the back door, I smelt the now-unfamiliar scent of a decent meal cooking – rabbit stew, if I wasn't mistaken – instead of our usual vegetable soup. A fire was roaring in the hearth, candles were flickering, and the farmhouse seemed almost as cosy as it had been before the war. To cap it all, there was music playing on Papa's gramophone – Vera Lynn's poignant 'We'll Meet Again'. Papa had managed to get hold of a copy of this just before we were occupied. It's my absolute favourite.

'Mama,' I smiled, finding her by the bread oven in the kitchen and gathering her into a hug. 'What's the occasion? Is this all for Sabine?'

'Not just Sabine. We're having some other guests round for supper tonight. Papa and I are sick of not being able to offer our hospitality to friends any more.'

Like excited schoolgirls, Sabine and I rushed off to wash our hands and faces and change our clothes. I've run out of rouge and lipstick but I have a little scent left, so we daubed ourselves with that and powdered our noses. Noelle came into my bedroom, unusually giddy with the thrill of it all and I let her have a squirt of scent, too. She wouldn't have needed any make-up even if I'd had any – she's a true beauty, my sister. We've both been blessed with a natural curl and our hair is a sort of brown-red ('auburn', Albert calls it), but while I've got what Mama calls a 'cheerful' face, Noelle's is exquisite. She always looks regal and serene, even when she's peeling spuds. She's certainly too pretty to work on the farm and I don't say that with any resentment; it's just the way it is. She was supposed to take over from me when I began at Odette's but she didn't have the muscle, so she helps Mama out in the house instead and Papa's got a couple of young lads helping him. I always lend a hand with the afternoon milking, too.

Mind you, these days running the house is almost as hard as working on the farm. Noelle's forever boiling beets in the big copper in the wash house to make sugar-beet syrup, as sugar is so hard to come by, and roasting parsnips to make coffee, as well as foraging for firewood now that fuel is limited. I help her out when I can, especially with the boring task of boiling potatoes for the pigs in the *chaudièthes* – our great big cauldrons.

Anyway, I digress . . . The next bit of excitement was the sound of a cork being pulled as we entered the kitchen.

'Papa! Wine! I had no idea we had any left.'

'A few bottles, and some champagne for when we're finally free again.'

I looked at the floor when he said this. Papa's so resolute, but we're all beginning to wonder when any of this will ever end. Soon, though, my spirits were soaring. The other guests arrived – Mr and Mrs Ecobichon, which gave me the opportunity to quiz them about Albert, though they had no more news than I did of his whereabouts. I was hoping they might have received a message through the Red Cross, as they did a little while back, but no luck. I sent a message to Albert using this service ages ago but I've heard nothing back yet.

At least I could reminisce with them about days gone by and I hungrily lapped up tales of Albert as a baby, a child, a teenager and a resolute young man ready to volunteer for service in the Royal Air Force. While we were talking about this, Mrs Ecobichon started rummaging around in her handbag and then pressed something into my hand. I looked at it and my heart jumped for joy: a photograph of Albert!

'Oh, I can't!' I said. 'It's too precious!'

'We had two copies made, my dear. It was before he left. And before the Germans invaded and banned all cameras. You have this one. You can talk to him that way. It's what I do,' she admitted, looking a little embarrassed.

I looked at the picture. There he was, my handsome sweetheart; all kitted out in his brand-new RAF uniform just before he'd left the island. His dark fringe was covering one eye and he was smiling. Unlike most photographs I'd come across, where the person in the picture looked dreadfully solemn, there was a real spark to that grin. It was a gift like no other.

'Thank you,' I said. 'It means so much.'

And then – surprise – Mrs Lucas from the farm next door arrived with a young man in tow. He looked vaguely familiar, yet I couldn't quite place him.

'Don't worry,' Mama told him. 'You're among friends here. No one will tell the authorities about you. And if there's a knock at the door, you can hide in the cellar.'

Oleg. It was Oleg! It had only been a little more than a week since I'd found him in the lane and yet he looked so different! Still thin as a rake but wearing proper warm clothes and with boots on his feet. He was smiling and there was a hint of light in those brilliant eyes. I couldn't help myself. I ran up to him and hugged him. I think he was a bit surprised to start with but then he hugged me back. 'Thank you, thank you, thank you,' he muttered in a strong Russian accent.

It was hard for Oleg to join in the conversation, though at one point during the evening he started to speak in Russian about his experience at the hands of the Germans. Papa began translating as best he could, telling us a story of treatment so dreadful I wanted to cover my ears. We learned how one particular officer – high up the ranks and with a scar across his face: probably the Grim One – had visited the Organisation Todt camp regularly and had been particularly vile to Oleg, humiliating him as well as being physically violent, as if he weren't suffering enough as a result of starvation, lack of sanitation and gruelling slave labour. But as Oleg became more and more upset, it was hard for Papa to keep up. In the end, Papa got up from the table and embraced Oleg to calm him. It seemed to help, anyway: after supper, Oleg sat contentedly enough by the fire and played with Lenny the farm cat and then listened with teary eyes while Noelle played stirring tunes on the piano. She's got a real talent for it and with the exception of Oleg, who didn't know the words, we were all defiantly singing along to 'Land of Hope and Glory' and 'I Vow to Thee, My Country'.

It turns out that Papa had spoken to Mrs Lucas and asked if she'd take Oleg in and hide him for a little while. Mrs Lucas is ever such a nice lady – a lonely widow, and very brave – so she agreed. She's grateful for the company and a bit of help around the house, though Oleg daren't go outside and help on the farm – much as he'd like to. I only hope that she – and Oleg – will be safe.

It's now almost midnight and it really has been a magical evening – a gift from times gone by and, I hope, a tiny taster of what life might one day become again. I go to sleep tonight with a full tummy and, aside from missing Albert, feeling truly happy.

Chapter Nine

CANTERBURY, DECEMBER 2016

LIBERTY

'Everything okay?' asked Alf.

Libby didn't look up. She was sitting at the dining table, scrolling through her phone and trying to remember the names of various caterers she'd been recommended by friends. 'Dad, what's your Wi-Fi password?'

'My what?'

'You know, for the Internet?'

'Oh, there's a problem with that. I haven't got a computer but Tink's got a laptop thingymejiggy for her writing. She said the Wi-Fi was "down" or something. The man's coming to fix it next week, I think. I've got a telephone directory, if that would help?'

'Thanks, but I need caterers in Jersey. This isn't going to be easy. I'll try to get online without Wi-Fi, but if I can't, I may need to ring a few friends. Do you mind?'

'Fire away. I'll be out in my veggie patch – at least until the snow starts anyway.'

'Snow? I thought it was meant to rain!'

'Oh, haven't you heard? It's being driven in from the Arctic, apparently. They're forecasting it for this afternoon and for the best part of the next week. You come and find me when you're done.'

But it all took so long to try and fail to find a network, then to ring a series of friends, and finally to try their recommended caterers, that by the time she'd finished – having thankfully found someone who was free and given them Amy's details – it was dark. Alf had finished in the garden and had lit the fire. Tink's physio had left, too, and the two of them were sitting side by side on the sofa, a bottle of sherry and three small glasses at the ready as they waited patiently for Libby's endless phone calls to come to an end.

'I'm so sorry . . .' Libby began.

'Doesn't matter a bit,' Tink said, patting the armchair next to her. 'Now, come and have a drink with us and tell us why you're here.'

'Mum, I'm here because of you! Your wrist. To help . . .'

'Nonsense. You know I'm perfectly capable. There's something else you're not telling us.'

Libby sat back against the chair, her head resting against a peanut-shaped cushion. It was surprisingly comfortable. She thought she might actually talk. Really talk. Pour out to her parents all of her anxieties, just like her own children did with her (well, the older two, anyway). But while Alf continued to wait peacefully for a response, it was too much for Tink, who had her own news.

'Oh, Libby, have I told you what happened about our old neighbours in Jersey? Remember Mrs Lucas – the lovely old duck who'd always lived next door? Almost a hundred when she died, poor thing. Can't think of anything worse than being old and infirm for so long. Dreadful. Anyway, she'd never had any children but she left her house to a younger man she'd had a soft spot for. He was nearly eighty himself, though, and died a year after he moved in! So then the farmhouse went up for sale for the first time in forever and these absolutely ghastly people moved in, do you remember? You went and had a little look when it was on the market – sent me pictures! Nouveau riche, those people were! They ripped out every little bit of history and installed a horrid minimal kitchen and those horrific plasmic TVs on the walls!'

'Plasma, Mum, not plasmic!' Libby laughed.

'Whatever. Anyway, they did all that and I've just heard from Ella Coutanche that they've sold up! Can you believe it? The next lot are even worse, apparently. Lots of stupidly enormous vehicles parked out the front and playing loud music every night. Never thought that would happen in L'Etacq. We're better off here, aren't we, Alf?'

'Oh, yes,' Alf replied, smiling faintly. 'Much better.'

Libby loved how her parents unrelentingly made the best of any situation, justifying to themselves that it had all worked out just as it was meant to when in reality they must still miss their own Jersey farmhouse terribly. Alf had lived there all his life until the move to Canterbury, as far as Libby was aware. She had so many fond memories of the place. It had been the cosiest house she'd ever known and in the most perfect seaside position. Libby remembered how thrilled she'd been when she'd married Henry and returned with him not just to her homeland but so close to the old farmhouse, where she'd found herself once again beguiled by the engaging landscapes and seascapes.

But somewhere along the line, since she'd become so preoccupied with her job and her children and being a vicar's wife, perhaps she'd started to take it slightly for granted. *I'm not going to any more*, Libby promised herself. And she realised that already, within the first day, this trip away was doing her good. Perhaps she just needed a bit of distance to get her back on track.

A moment later her phone rang.

'Hello?'

'Mum, it's me,' came a small voice at the other end. She nearly fainted with shock. It was Milo! Milo never, ever rang her. If he *had* to communicate with her it was via text message and they could win prizes for their curtness.

'Darling! Milo! Are you okay?' she asked. All her alarm bells were ringing.

'Erm, not really. Dad told me I had to call you. I've been sent home from school.'

'Why? Are you ill?' Immediately, she imagined the worst. He'd been to the doctor and received an instant diagnosis of something life-threatening.

'No, nothing like that. It's a bit embarrassing. I, um, I was caught on my phone during Maths.'

Was that all? The relief! 'Well, why did they send you home for that? Surely a telling-off would have sufficed!'

'Mrs Le Maistre took my phone off me and had a look at what I'd been texting. It was just a message to Chelsea but it was a bit rude.'

'How rude?'

'Um, just kind of . . .'

Clearly Milo was too mortified to go into details. 'Put your father on the phone,' Libby said in her sternest voice.

'Henry! What on earth?'

'He was caught sexting,' Henry whispered, having clearly taken the phone through to another room. 'Libby, the things he said in the message. There were some terms I didn't even know myself! I had to look them up! He swears it's all talk and no action and let's just hope that's true.'

'Oh, Henry, this is dreadful! I'll come home, get a flight tomorrow.'

But Henry surprised her. 'No, don't,' he said, firmly. 'This whole business has been a bit of a wake-up call for Milo, I think, and he's finally opening up to me. I think I can get him talking, properly, and it might change the dynamic if you come back.'

Libby felt instantly offended and – the worst thing for a mother – unnecessary. But then she realised that, for once, Henry had lifted his head out of the sand to deal with an issue to do with the children. And if he was having some success with Milo, it would be daft to sabotage that.

'Well, if you're sure,' she replied. 'But if things change and you need me or Milo needs me, just let me know, okay, and I'll be straight over. What about the school? Do I need to speak to them? Is he suspended?'

'No, fortunately not. He was just sent home for the rest of the day and I've been ordered to confiscate his phone. I've managed to placate the Head, so I don't think you need to get involved. Chelsea's phone was confiscated, too, and her messages were even ruder, so they've both just been given a jolly good telling-off. Look, I'd better go. Milo said he'd like to do some jamming with me of all things, so I need to tune my guitar! Heaven help us. I'll call you tomorrow. Don't worry!'

Libby turned off her phone. She was trembling. How had those innocent little newborn bundles she'd been passed at the start of their lives grown up to be so much trouble? 'Don't worry,' Henry had said, but how could she not?

'What's happened?' asked Tink, refilling Libby's glass with sherry. Libby downed it in one.

'That's my girl,' said Tink. 'Now do tell!'

Libby sat back in her chair and closed her eyes for a moment, feeling the sweet burn of the sherry in her throat. Her father rose quietly from the sofa and dropped another log on the fire. The shot of alcohol and the comforting sounds – ticking clock, gently crackling hearth – should have soothed her, but it was no good.

After Libby had explained it all, Tink burst out laughing. 'What a naughty boy!' she exclaimed, with an inappropriately proud look on her face. Alf abandoned his drink and came to sit down next to Libby on the arm of her chair. He took his daughter's hand in his own – a big, strong hand patterned with liver spots.

'It's like Julian of Norwich said: "All shall be well, and all shall be well, and all manner of thing shall be well." My mum used to tell me that when I was worried.'

Libby smiled a small smile and lent into him for a hug. 'Thanks, Dad,' she said, and she realised that, if she couldn't be at home with Milo, then she was in the next best place. It would be hard to beat the comfort of a pearl of wisdom and a cuddle from her dad.

Chapter Ten

Jersey, December 1941

Queenie's journal

Less than three weeks until Christmas now, not that any of us need much time to prepare for it as we would have done in years gone by. After all, there's little we can buy in the way of presents and there'll be no tree this year or feast to prepare, though Papa is still promising a pig. When I'm not working at the salon, my spare moments are filled with rehearsals for the pantomime. Thank heavens; if it weren't for that, I'd be bored stiff.

The Germans are heavily into censorship, so we're putting on *Cinderella*, thinking it would be an innocuous enough choice, but when a couple of officers turned up during rehearsal this afternoon they told Buttons his costume was too similar to the British army uniform (it isn't), so now we've got to change his outfit. Poor Diane – our wardrobe lady – has enough to do, though thankfully she wants to keep herself busy. She's a pretty young widow, from the East End of London originally, but according to Mama her husband was an absolute brute, so she may well be better off without him – though obviously not financially. Since her husband passed away, Diane has made ends meet working as a seamstress. After she'd saved enough to pay for the family's evacuation, she sent her young children across to the mainland on what turned out to be one of the last boats, to stay with a cousin. She'd planned on joining them a week later once she'd packed up the house but by then the Germans had arrived and there was no escape. She'd been distraught, beside herself. So Mama told her about our drama club and suggested she try to keep herself busy by helping us out with costumes. 'You keep yourself occupied, my love, and before you know it, you'll be reunited with those darlings of yours,' Mama reassured her.

Diane is ever so good at costumes. We're delighted to have her help, so it's one of those nice arrangements that benefits everyone. She's made me a cracker of a dress out of some old curtains and I look like a real trout in it – purposefully, as I'm an Ugly Sister. Her dress for the Fairy Godmother is a masterpiece as well – Tommy doesn't half look the part. He's an absolute hoot – truly, he makes the show. It's not so much what he says – he's so hard to understand, as always – but rather all the daft expressions he pulls. It'll be a lovely bit of light relief for everyone over the Christmas period. Mind you, not that Tommy's own mood is lightened by the performance. He was hopping mad when the German officers turned up, sticking their noses in.

'*Mouôn Doue d'la vie!* What business is it of theirs what we get up to here, putting on a harmless pantomime, eh? They should keep their dirty, rotten Nazi beaks out of it . . .' he'd seethed in the wings while Foxy, the young chap in charge of our drama club, calmly dealt with the officers, promising them that of course the outfit would be changed. He's called Foxy due to his orange hair and rather too-long nose, beneath which he sports a matching orange moustache. He's a very odd sort of chap, though utterly lovely.

Tommy, however, isn't quite as impressed with Foxy. 'He should grow a bloody backbone, eh, that little carrot-topped boy! He's letting himself be *débraiesi* by the Jerries!'

As ever with Tommy, I looked a bit blank at the last part of his outburst. 'Henpecked!' he virtually shouted now, his face puce with anger. 'Henpecked like a coward who lets himself be bossed around by his dragon of a wife!'

I must confess, I did stop listening at this point. Tommy is hilarious as an actor but he becomes a little wearing with his antiquated views and his quick temper.

Anyway, after the rehearsal – we can't do evenings due to the wretched curfew – and despite Tommy's outburst, I was feeling quite light-hearted cycling home, until I came across Mary Jane and the German officer I realised must be her fancy man. They were along one of the little lanes towards home and I thought they were canoodling at first, though as I got closer I could see Mary Jane was crying and her red lipstick was all smudged. The braids in her hair were falling down and she had bloodshot eyes and terribly puffy cheeks. I felt bad for her then, even if she was wearing a fur stole purloined from a requisitioned house. Maybe she'd got herself into a situation she couldn't get herself out of. Perhaps I could help her? But the Grim One looked pretty grim, just as Tommy had said, and I didn't fancy crossing him. He was in an officer's uniform – a great grey coat, cap and smart black boots – and had a moustache just like Hitler's, a nasty pallid complexion and that scar across his face I'd heard tell of. I didn't like the look of him at all.

There was something about the whole scene that made me feel out of sorts, though I couldn't quite pinpoint what the problem was – obviously aside from the fact that a German was walking out with one of my old friends. I didn't feel right all evening. Mama couldn't understand it – I'm usually the chatty one at dinner. But Noelle had been stirred to animation by some interesting news, so she entertained Mama and Papa for once. She was telling us about Sybil, whose mother, Violet, is headmistress at one of the village schools (we always call it 'Violet's school' to distinguish it from the other one). Apparently, she and her parents are hiding one of our Jewish friends, Rachel Weider.

Rachel's father has already been killed in Poland and her English mother is missing. The poor thing had been traumatised enough by these events before having the island that had since become her home invaded by her father's murderers. When she fled Poland, she came to Jersey to stay with her great-uncle, thinking it would be the safest place to be. But it turned out the old uncle was a bit of a letch, so she left him as quick as she could. She did ever so well for herself – managed to get herself a job as a typist and found some nice accommodation in St Peter. Noelle and Sybil met her shortly before we were occupied and they quickly befriended her as she's one of those rare sorts: softly spoken and gentle, yet with a great sense of humour.

'So that's why you couldn't track her down when we went to the cinema . . . Sybil kept it quiet, didn't she? She never said that Rachel was staying with her.'

'No, Rachel was just keeping a low profile then, I think, deciding what to do. This only happened yesterday and Sybil's been sworn to secrecy about it,' Noelle replied. 'But she couldn't keep it from me. It's a real saga. Apparently the poor girl's been in a right state since all the Jews were told they had to register themselves. She thought she'd better do it but then as soon as she did she wished she hadn't. She was terrified she'd be deported. So yesterday she decided to feign suicide by leaving her clothes, shoes and identity card down by the sea and then begged Sybil to let her hide in the school attics.'

Papa looked alarmed. 'Well, if the Germans aren't convinced about the suicide we'll hear about it soon enough: there'll be a notice in the *Evening Post* about her. I'll have to keep an eye out.' He sighed. 'A brave but risky business for Sybil's family. Like Mrs Lucas, it's hard living with the stress of hiding someone and trying to feed an extra person without a ration card. We'll smuggle them some food. Noelle, you mustn't

Rebecca Boxall

breathe a word of this to anyone.' He was stern, and Noelle said of course she wouldn't, though she's so ditzy sometimes, I'm not surprised Papa was worried.

Noelle was most unlike herself all evening, in a state of great excitement: her high cheekbones were aflame and she seemed almost delirious as she told us this highly sensitive tale. I hope she's all right. She's asleep beside me now, but she's very restless and her face still looks red. I feel so uneasy I'm not sure I'll be able to get to sleep.

Chapter Eleven

Canterbury, December 2016

Liberty

Libby woke of her own accord, relishing the joy of not being rudely disturbed by the alarm on her phone, though she immediately checked it while she opened the bedroom curtains, to see if she'd received a text from Stella. Nothing. She needed to find a quiet moment to speak to Alf about it all.

She padded downstairs in her slippers and dressing gown and found Alf and Tink sitting at the dining table – always laid for breakfast the night before – contentedly engrossed in the morning papers while sipping tea from dainty china teacups. Libby couldn't help smiling. Who nowadays would drink tea served from a pot in delicate china cups every morning?

'Good morning!' smiled Tink, quickly jumping up to kiss her daughter. She smelt lovely – of rose-scented shampoo and freshly brewed Darjeeling. 'Sit down, I'll just get your brekkie,' she said. 'And don't start fussing about my wrist! I'm fine!' she added, before hurrying through to the kitchen to produce the same breakfast she'd been offering for decades: half a grapefruit followed by a boiled egg with soldiers. The predictability of it all was so heavenly that Libby could feel her tension melting away.

Alf looked across at Libby. 'You know, Libs, when you were a little girl, you were so absorbed by the outside world. So curious and interested; not inward-looking at all. Haven't you noticed? Something that would've had you enthralled as a girl? Have a good look.'

Libby did. She looked all around the room and didn't notice anything remarkable, until finally she realised what Alf was talking about. She stepped slowly towards the living-room window and put her hand to it, the cold pane a stark contrast to the warmth of the interior. Outside, the whole world was blanketed in white. How on earth had she not noticed it when she'd pulled open the curtains in her bedroom? She turned to Alf and smiled. '*Snow!*' she squealed and she ran across the room to hug him.

Libby spent most of the day out in the snow with Alf, larking about just as they'd always done when she was a child. By nine o'clock that evening she was exhausted but compared with the kind of exhaustion she usually felt, this was very different. Not that horrible, stressed-out kind of tiredness, but instead a pleasant sleepiness born of fresh air and exercise.

Tink made Libby a mug of Horlicks and she took the drink up to bed, sank under the covers and, before she'd finished half of it, she dozed off. She slept solidly until eight the following morning. By then, Alf and Tink were well and truly stuck into the day, Alf busy shovelling snow from the front path and Tink pushing the Hoover around the living room with her good hand while singing along to tunes playing on Radio 2. When she spotted Libby, she quickly turned off the vacuum cleaner.

'Now that's better,' she said, looking up at her daughter. 'Two decent nights' sleep and no more dark shadows under those lovely eyes of yours! I've always thought hazel eyes need sleep to stay sparkly. You know, Ella Coutanche was telling me that lilac is the best colour to wear on your lids if you've got hazel eyes. Have I told you that already?'

Libby grinned. 'No, but I'll bear it in mind – thanks, Mum. In fact, I need some new eyeshadow. And mascara. Actually, I need quite a few things, not to mention Christmas presents.' She sat down and started to scoop the little segments of flesh from her halved grapefruit. 'It's so unlike me. I've usually bought and wrapped everything by the end of November.'

'Well, why don't we head into the city this morning?' suggested Tink gleefully. Tink was an absolute shopaholic. She always had been – even when she'd lived in L'Etacq, she'd driven into town once a week for a good bargain hunt (she was only ever interested in 'deals'), but Canterbury was heaven for the likes of Tink: so much choice, so many sales. 'There's a sale on in Debenhams and you could probably get all your prezzies in there! I'll be your helper, like a little elf! Luckily, I bought all of mine before the accident.'

'What about the snow, though? I suppose we could put on some sturdy boots and walk . . .'

'And cart all those heavy bags back? With my bad wrist? No, Dad will take us. He won't mind . . .'

'What won't I mind?' asked Alf, as he slammed the front door and, after taking off his boots, plodded through to the living room.

'Driving us into the city,' Tink said, turning round and treating him to her most winning smile.

Alf sucked his teeth. 'Ooh, I don't know about that. The snow's pretty thick.'

'Oh, the truck will be fine!' Tink told him, dismissing his concerns. 'Tell you what, dear, you go and do all that de-icing and warming up or what have you and Libby will quickly get herself ready, then we can head off before it gets too busy. Or do you want an egg?' Tink asked Libby, concern at ensuring her daughter was well fed pushing aside her excitement for a moment.

'No, a grapefruit will do me nicely. I'm trying to lose weight. Give me five minutes to shower and dress and I'll be with you.'

As promised, she was hopping into the back of the truck five minutes later. She was about to get her phone out to while away the slow journey into the city but, as the truck turned right onto Rheims Way, she checked herself, leaving it in her bag and just enjoying the sights.

Alf was the slowest of drivers at the best of times. He always wore leather driving gloves and every manoeuvre was painfully deliberate. He was courteous, though, always waving to thank anyone who might let him out. Given the snow, it took an absolute age to arrive in the city centre but as soon as they did, Tink and Libby were off with shouts of 'See you later!' and 'We'll call and let you know when we need picking up!' Alf tooted his horn and slowly departed.

'Where to?' asked Libby.

'Let's start with Debenhams,' suggested Tink, clearly itching to see what their sale had to offer. They made their way through the store's electric doors and instantly needed to take off their thick coats and drape them over their arms, as the heating was on overdrive thanks to the cold weather.

'Make-up first then,' said Tink, and, once Libby was stocked up with her cosmetics, they headed through to the gift department, where she managed to find presents for all the family and her godchildren, too.

'Goodness, these bags are heavy,' Libby said, struggling under the weight of her many purchases.

'I've got an idea. Hang on a sec!' Tink said, and she approached a startled-looking young man behind one of the tills and persuaded him to let them leave their bags with him for a few hours so they could continue their shopping unencumbered.

'We must remember to pick them up later!' Libby laughed. 'Shall we go and have a coffee?' She was gasping but Tink wasn't done yet.

'Let's just have a little look in the clothes department . . .' she said, and hurried towards the lift. Tink was an absolute dervish to shop with

– she picked up bundles and bundles of garments to try on (piling them onto her good arm on this occasion), always managing to bag herself the largest changing room and then, usually so fastidious, she would just walk out, leaving everything she didn't want to buy in a heap on the stool or chair.

'Mum, you need to put things back on their hangers and give them to the lady!' Libby whispered but Tink brushed aside her admonishment.

'But the ladies don't mind doing it!' she said, her eyes wide and earnest. 'It's more interesting than standing there handing out tokens!'

Despite her enthusiasm, by the end of her trying-on marathon Tink hadn't fixed on buying anything because the truth was, though shopping was her great passion, she couldn't actually afford to indulge it. But despite this, she hadn't left everything discarded in the changing room. She'd clung on to one item: a charcoal-grey cape with a paler grey faux-fur collar. When she'd tried it on, she'd looked a million dollars – the grey contrasting beautifully with her cropped white hair – but it had been far too expensive. Eventually, with a look of regret, she'd carefully placed it back on the rail on the shop floor.

After their coffee, while Tink went to the ladies', Libby raced back to the fashion department and quickly bought the cape for Tink as a Christmas present, before stowing the extra bag with the stunned-looking guardian of her other purchases and quickly darting back to the ladies' before Tink realised what she was up to.

After Debenhams, they hit the streets and meandered along, nipping into boutiques housed within ancient Tudor buildings. They crossed the bridge over the River Stour and paused to look at the medieval ducking stool that jutted out over the water beside the Old Weavers' House – a half-timbered construction that was now home to a nice-looking restaurant.

'Didn't they used to duck witches there or something?' asked Libby, remembering the police officer she and Stella had nicknamed 'PC Witch' when she'd started a false rumour about Libby being pregnant when in fact she'd just put on a bit of weight. Stella had been absolutely incensed and ended up making the woman stand up in the middle of the canteen to admit she'd made the whole thing up.

'Yes – suspected witches. They'd nab one and dunk her for several minutes. If she didn't drown, she was proved a witch. If she did drown, then her name was cleared but by then she was dead! Rather lose–lose! Not only witches, though. It was used to punish "scolds", too.'

'Scolds?'

'Women who would talk back at their husbands too much! Imagine!'

Libby shook her head. 'Makes you glad to be a woman nowadays, anyway. Look – shall we eat at the Old Weavers'? Let me treat you to lunch there.' She checked her watch. 'Gosh, it's already gone one.'

'Ooh, lovely,' Tink said, her eyes lighting up. She loved eating out, especially at smart-looking places like the Old Weavers'.

'How are the children?' she asked, once she'd settled herself down and cast a quick glance at the menu. 'Apart from naughty Milo!'

'The same as always. Liam's gorgeous and fragile and worrying. Convinced he's going to make a million one minute, out partying all night the next, then in the depths of despair. And so the cycle continues . . .'

'Has he got a girlfriend?'

They were interrupted by a waiter, who took their order with a stubby pencil produced from behind his ear. Libby ordered a half bottle of wine for them as well, and the chap quickly returned to pour their drinks.

'Thank you,' she said, then returned her attention to Tink. 'No one serious. He only seems to be capable of flings. At least there's not likely to be another wedding in the family for a while!'

'Ah yes, Amy! How's she getting on?'

'Let's just say the wedding preparations aren't bringing out the best in her!' Libby said, and Tink laughed, knowing Amy well enough not to need any further explanation.

'And Henry?' Tink asked, taking a sip of wine and closing her eyes momentarily in utter bliss. Wine at lunchtime was a rare treat.

'He's fine. You know, busy as always.'

'I don't know how you put up with it. That job. It pays a pittance and look how much he puts into it, poor man!'

'Oh, you don't need to feel sorry for him, Mum, he loves it!'

'And you don't.' It wasn't a question, but a recognition of Libby's feelings.

Libby smiled in a resigned sort of fashion. 'You know I don't but I'm not going to make him change careers for me.'

'You put up with things. You always have. I remember our move to Canterbury. You had your father and I fooled that you were perfectly happy about it all. It took Stella to tell us how distraught you were – how much you missed Jersey. How is she? You haven't mentioned her! Are you still thick as thieves?'

Libby groaned inwardly at the mention of her oldest friend. 'Mum, we've fallen out.'

Tink looked aghast. 'What? But you don't fall out. You've never fallen out!'

'Well, we have this time.'

'But what about?'

Libby sighed. She sat back in her chair and drained her glass of wine, looking out of the window at the river beyond. Droopy willow trees dipped their tangled branches into the rushing water. She was about to explain when her phone started to ring.

'Sorry,' she said, delving into her handbag and rummaging for it. 'I'll just turn this bloody thing off.' But then she saw it was Henry's number. 'It's Henry. I'll tell him I'll call back later . . . Hen, I'll call you back, if that's okay? I'm just having lunch with Mum. It's so festive here with all the snow!'

'Gosh! It's mild as anything here,' Henry said. 'The daffodils are out! But look, Libby, don't go just yet – you need to hear this.'

Oh, heavens, what now? She repeated the thought aloud: 'Oh, heavens, what now?'

'It's Amy . . .'

Chapter Twelve

Jersey, December 1941

Queenie's Journal

I woke up at three o'clock in the morning. For some reason, the sheets felt drenched.

'Noelle! Noelle!' I gasped, shaking my sister, but she was like a rag doll. She groaned in response to my prodding. I placed my palm on her forehead and found she was boiling hot. I realised she was horribly unwell. I lit a candle and clambered out of bed, rushing through to Papa and Mama's room.

'Mama! Mama, it's Noelle. She's ill. Come quickly!' I whispered, and she followed me through to our bedroom. Mama immediately crossed herself when she saw the state Noelle was in.

'Queenie, go and get me a flannel and some cold water. Quickly, my love.'

I ran downstairs, rushing outside to collect a bucket of water, then heaving it upstairs, trying not to slosh the liquid onto the floor as I lugged it through to the bedroom. Then I grabbed a cloth and, after dampening it, passed it to Mama.

'Does she need a doctor?' Papa asked, having been woken by all the commotion.

'Yes, I'm afraid so. It looks like scarlet fever to me. Her tongue's all red and bumpy,' Mama replied. I immediately thought of Beth in *Little Women* and felt sick with panic. 'But of course Dr Harrison returned to the mainland just before the occupation. Worried the Germans would end up deporting anyone who wasn't local, poor man. There's not another doctor in the village, is there?'

'No . . . the only other one I know is Dr Le Gresley but he's in town. I've got his number. I'll give him a call,' Papa said. A few minutes later, he returned to the bedroom. 'Bad news. The telephone line's down, so I'm going to have to cycle into town. I'd take the truck but there's a better chance of me getting away with being out after curfew if I cycle. Besides, there's barely any petrol left. I've hidden it in the barn.'

'I'll go,' I said immediately. 'Papa, I'll be quicker.'

Papa wasn't keen on that idea but one look at Noelle was enough to convince him. He gave me the address and I stored it in my memory. 'Just be careful, my darling. Now I'm going to be worrying about both of you.'

'I'll be as quick as I can,' I promised him, and I began to dress in my warmest clothes and hurried outside to find my bicycle. I pedalled furiously towards town, guided by the moon, and remembering to cycle on the right as we're now ordered to, though the spray of waves kept on soaking me as the tide was high.

I made it to town in just under an hour, speeding past the rat-house – the town hall, now the German HQ, has been renamed the *Rathaus* and has quickly picked up the obvious nickname. The swastika flag hanging from the building waved jeeringly at me. Just around the corner from there was Dr Le Gresley's home. But when I arrived there, his bleary-eyed wife told me her husband was attending to a woman in labour in St Lawrence. She was in the thick of it, apparently, and there was no way he'd be able to leave her. I felt like crying but I got back on my bicycle and began to pedal furiously homewards. It was just as I started winding my way up Le Vieux Beaumont that a car came out of nowhere. I stopped dead still. The driver slowed and wound down the window. I saw a man behind the wheel wearing that distinctive German uniform. My heart sank.

'You are out after curfew,' he remarked in a clipped accent. 'Do you have your identity card?'

'Yes,' I said, handing it over. 'I'm sorry,' I began to gabble. 'But it's my sister. She's really ill. I cycled all the way from St Ouen to town to find a doctor but he's busy, so I need to get home again as quickly as possible.'

The man looked at me long and hard. He had a serious face but his eyes weren't unkind. 'Get in,' he ordered. My legs quaked. 'Leave your bicycle there behind the hedge. I will pick it up for you later. You can direct me to your home. I will take a look at your sister for you.'

I looked at him, surprised.

'I am a doctor with the medical corps,' he explained. 'You are lucky.'

Lucky? I felt instantly resentful at that remark. After all, we were hardly lucky to have had our beautiful island taken over by a load of bullies who scared our own doctors away, came up with stupid rules and gave us silly curfews. But it was true enough that the outcome of my curfew breach could have been worse and it was a genuine stroke of luck that the man was a doctor: and one who spoke such good English.

Papa and Mama looked utterly horrified when I returned to the farmhouse with a German in tow instead of Dr Le Gresley, but they quickly composed themselves and showed him the way to the bedroom so that he could take a look at Noelle. I decided to cuddle up with Lenny the cat on the sofa in the living room, a blanket pulled over me for warmth, but I could hear low, urgent voices upstairs.

Sometime later, I heard the German leave. I went upstairs and found Mama stroking Noelle's hair. Papa was looking out of the window, his lovely face, with its fine handlebar moustache, watching the doctor drive off.

'How is she?' I asked. Noelle looked more peaceful, though her cheeks were still an angry red.

'It pays to be pretty,' Papa said as he lit up his pipe. Tobacco is scarce and he's rationing himself but he tends to reach for a smoke in times of worry. 'The doctor had just finished his shift at the hospital where he'd been tending to some of his lot with the same illness – scarlet fever. He took one look at Noelle and realised how unwell she was – he said she might well experience complications unless she received some medicine immediately. And, after his shift, he had some in his bag. He shouldn't have given it to us, but one look at that beautiful face and he did. He'll be in severe trouble if his superiors find out, so we mustn't breathe a word to anyone. She should be all right now, thank the Lord, but she'll need to keep taking the medicine for a few days and she'll be in bed for some weeks. You'll need to sleep in the little room, Queenie – this disease is horribly contagious.'

I nodded in agreement and we all stood round, silently watching Noelle. After a couple of minutes, I could bear it no more. 'If she's going to be all right, then why do you look so sad, Papa?' I asked, looking from him to Mama.

'He feels like a collaborator,' Mama explained. 'For taking medicine from a German.'

'But Noelle might have died if you hadn't!'

Papa didn't reply but he put an arm around me and squeezed my shoulder.

'And anyway,' I continued, 'there must be some good ones. Some of them, like that chap, are probably just as desperate about being in this situation as we are.'

But Papa wouldn't be comforted. He let his arm drop from my shoulder and left us, returning to his bedroom, smoke trailing behind him.

Chapter Thirteen

Canterbury, December 2016

Liberty

'Did you like him?' Tink asked as she and Libby made their way back to Debenhams to pick up their bags before meeting Alf. As they walked along, large flakes of snow began to fall from the steely sky, but Libby barely noticed.

'Jonty? Well, he's kind of . . . bland, if I'm honest. But he and Amy always seemed quite well suited. Not that Amy's bland, obviously. I mean, when she shouts "Jump!" Jonty asks "How high?"'

Tink giggled and clasped hold of Libby so they could walk arm in arm. 'So why do you think he's dumped her, then? Had enough of being bossed around?'

'To be truthful, I was a little bit worried this might happen. Amy's been completely obsessed with wedding preparations, competing with her friend Bethany, who's getting married around the same time, and I think she completely forgot the point of it all – that it's meant to be a celebration of their relationship.'

'So do you think it's final?'

'According to Henry it is. He thinks I need to fly home. Amy's devastated, apparently. She's even taken a couple of days off work. Unheard of.'

Tink tutted and pointed towards the Debenhams entrance. 'Well, don't go rushing home just yet,' she said. 'At least give it another night and see how the land lies tomorrow. It's too late now anyway and besides, Dad wants to take you to a service at the Cathedral tonight.'

Libby looked at Tink, surprised. 'He does?'

'I know, he's not usually one for religion but he's rather taken to the Cathedral in the last year or so. Says it makes him feel goosebumpy. I'm not sure if that's a good thing or not, but it's clearly not put him off. I'm not really *into* churches and whatnot, as you know, but I told him you'd go with him, if you don't mind? It's one of those Advent services, I think . . . A carol service in the nave.'

'Course I don't mind. It'll be lovely – really Christmassy. And a nice distraction from this latest drama.'

By now they were at the till and the boy, still looking like a rabbit in the headlights, quickly handed over their bags. They trooped out into the darkening afternoon, where the snowfall was gathering momentum.

'The visibility's getting pretty bad,' Alf said, when they'd clambered into the truck. 'Think we're better off walking tonight. Libby, I wondered if you'd come to a service with me? At the Cathedral?'

'Mum was telling me. Of course I will. How festive, to walk there in the snow.'

Back home, Alf quickly lit the fire while Tink prepared a light supper of scrambled eggs on toast, which they ate from trays on their laps watching *Antiques Roadshow*.

'Right – time we were off,' said Alf, once he'd taken their plates through to the kitchen.

'Let me just wash up first,' Libby said, jumping up to join him in the kitchen.

'No need for that,' Tink told her. 'I'm perfectly capable of doing it with one hand. Now off you go and trill along to all those lovely Christmas tunes. I'm going to put a nice old-fashioned film on – *Miracle on 34th Street* or something like that – and see how I get on wrapping prezzies one-handed!'

The flakes were still falling as they walked over the railway bridge, then through the wintery Westgate Gardens. It was absolutely freezing but also quite perfect: still and quiet, all sound muffled by the snow, which was settling heavily on every surface. As they trudged their frozen boots through Burgate, the snow glowed amber in the streetlight. Then they came upon the Cathedral – dramatically floodlit, it looked as if it were covered in white icing. It was stunning.

Inside, their feet began to thaw and they found themselves a free pew in the nave. Libby took a seat and looked up and around her, in awe of the surrounding grandeur: the soaring height of the stupendous stained-glass windows; the painstaking architectural detail. But most of all – her father was right – she noticed the feel of the place, especially once the service began: Libby felt a genuine reverence in taking part in it. The choir gave her goosebumps, just like Tink had said, from the little boy's angelic opening solo in 'Once in Royal David's City' to the thunderous final chorus of 'O Come All Ye Faithful'. Somehow, it felt completely different to being at church back in Jersey, where she felt as though she were always on duty, helping Henry cater to the needs of his flock, and never stopping for a moment to reflect on the meaning of it all and her own faith – which she'd found early on in her marriage with Henry and knew was still deeply buried inside her somewhere.

'Wow!' she exhaled, as they made their way out. Without discussing it, Libby and her father headed instinctively towards The Old Buttermarket, a nearby pub. 'I can see why you've taken to the place. Everyone uses the word "awesome" these days, but that really was.'

'It's special, isn't it? I knew you'd feel the same.'

Arriving in the warmth of the pub, Alf ordered a pint of ale for himself and a gin and tonic for Libby. She spotted a table and a couple of stools tucked into a corner, near the fire.

'At last – a moment to ourselves,' said Alf, carefully tucking his long legs under the table. 'Cheers! Now tell me, Libs, what on earth's going on? I don't mean with Milo and Amy and their silly dramas. I mean you.'

Libby felt her face flush. It seemed a little alien to have someone want to know about *her*. Not Libby the police officer or Libby the vicar's wife or Libby the mother, but just Libby. The person.

'I . . .' She faltered, then was mortified when she burst into tears. Alf took the outburst in his stride and handed over a large, freshly laundered handkerchief pulled from his trouser pocket. Libby blew her nose loudly and dabbed at her eyes. She took a deep breath. 'I'm so sorry,' she said. 'It's just . . . everything. It's all so trivial, really, but there's been so much pressure in every area of my life lately and then . . . Dad, I've fallen out with Stella.'

'Hmm,' he said, as though he wasn't surprised. 'Anything to do with her mother dying recently?'

Libby was startled. How did he know that was the beginning of it all? 'Yes, but how . . . ? How did you know? Did Mum say? I mentioned it to her earlier.'

'No. Just an educated guess,' said Alf. 'Thought it would all come out sooner or later and a deathbed's always the place where people get things off their chest, so they say. I heard she'd died – Sybil, Stella's mother. I'm not sure when the funeral's going to be but we won't be going. There was no love lost between our families, as you know.'

'Well, yes, we always knew that, Stella and I. But we never knew *why*. Why did you never tell us the history? The reason behind the friction between our families? I remember making friends with Stella at the Christmas party in my first year of school, and coming home to tell you and Mum all about her. I couldn't put my finger on it at that age but somehow I knew I hadn't done quite the right thing. You should have told us the reason.'

Alf sighed and took a glug of ale. He slowly placed the pint glass down on the table. 'We didn't want to stop you being friends with her and obviously her parents didn't feel they could do anything about it either. I think we all thought the friendship wouldn't last, but you proved us wrong. You're right, of course – we should at some point have explained about the animosity. But it's a Jersey thing. You sweep things under the carpet. You don't talk about the difficult past if you can help it. You try to forget – to get on with things.'

'But Dad, what was it all about? All she told me was that my grand-parents had done something terrible to Sybil and her parents.'

'Interesting,' was all Alf said. He patted Libby on the shoulder and pottered off to the bar to get them another round. Libby waited impatiently for him to return.

'So?' she said. 'Is it true? What on earth did they do?'

Alf sighed and rubbed his eyes. 'No, no it's not true. But it's no good me trying to explain it to you. I'll forget important bits. There's a journal at home. Your great-aunt Queenie kept one for a short period during the occupation and it makes for fascinating reading. That'll give you the answers you're looking for.'

'But Dad, I can't wait that long! I need to know now!'

'Why? What's the hurry, Libs? Always in a rush, you are, nowadays. Not just you, either – your whole generation and the one after you, too. Instant gratification. But you know, there's a pleasure and satisfaction to be had in anticipation.'

'But what if I need to fly back to Jersey tomorrow to sort Amy out?'

'Then you can take the diary with you but please – whatever you do – don't lose it. It's rather precious. Queenie never had any children of her own, so it was passed down to me when she died all those years ago, shortly after my mother. You remember Queenie – she was a wonderful woman. Full of spark – an adventurous spirit. And an avid reader. She got me interested in reading, actually, as a young boy. And I passed that love on to you. Are you still a bookworm?'

'I am usually but I've lost my Kindle, so I haven't been able to read anything for weeks!'

Alf shook his head. He obviously thought she was a lost cause. 'Well, maybe that's just as well. The journal will be something to read while you're with us. And don't give me any more claptrap about rushing back to Jersey. I'll wager you a fiver that daughter of yours will ring up in the morning to tell you she's made up with love's young dream,' Alf said, with a rare cheeky smile.

The next morning, Libby pulled herself out of bed and – before checking her phone – pulled open the curtains and took in the beautiful fresh layer of snow that covered the road. Only then did she check for messages.

Hi Mum, all sorted out with Jonty. He's such a pig sometimes but he's apologised and I've decided to forgive him. Wedding's back on. Dad said to text you. Caterers you found sound okay – think we'll have to go with them. Can you call me tonight to discuss menus? Thanks x

Libby rolled her eyes and laughed. Why were her parents always bloody well right?

Chapter Fourteen

Jersey, December 1941

Queenie's journal

By the grace of God, no one else has been struck down with the fever – a great mercy, since it seems unlikely any of the rest of us would stand a chance of obtaining any medicine. According to Papa, it's called 'penicillin' – a new treatment and exceptionally difficult to get hold of. In fact, Papa says the Germans haven't even worked out how to make it, so he thinks one of the medics must have a British connection who's helping them obtain medication for the troops.

The German doctor has been to see Noelle several times since he first treated her. Papa doesn't like it but what can he do? And I've soon come to realise the man is actually not much more than a boy, despite his medical training – only a couple of years older than me, I think, and he seems genuinely concerned for Noelle. Yesterday, I was sitting at the bureau in the living room, writing to Albert with Lenny the cat on my lap, when I heard his voice behind me.

'That's a lovely cat. You should be careful. Some of the soldiers are saying that if food runs out and they get too hungry they'll . . .' He seemed to think better of finishing this sentence.

'Can I help?' I asked, frowning. 'Is it Noelle? Is she all right?'

He smiled and I noticed he has the kind of face that alters dramatically with a smile, lighting up. 'She is doing very well,' he responded. 'She is teasing me. She thinks my name is very stupid.'

'What is it?' I asked. 'Your name?'

'Wolfgang Krause,' he admitted sheepishly. '*Kraus* means "curly-haired". You can see I am a true Krause,' he said, pointing to his blond curls.

I smiled, too – I couldn't help it – and waited to see what it was he wanted.

'I couldn't help notice the books lined up along the windowsill in the bedroom you share with your sister. Noelle told me they're yours. I was wondering . . . I have no books with me here and I miss them so much. I could use the library but my senior officer does not approve of the place. Could I . . . ? I don't suppose I could borrow one? I would take great care of it, I promise, and return it to you very quickly.'

I hesitated. I felt much like Papa had when he'd accepted the medicine for Noelle from Wolfgang. Was it collaborating to lend him my books? But then I put such thoughts from my head. Here was a young man not much older than me with a shared interest in reading. How could I deny him such a simple request when he might well have saved my sister's life?

'Which one would you like to read first?' I asked, and he smiled again.

'If you don't mind, I should very much like to try Dickens. I have heard so much about his writing but I've never read any English novels. Which one should I start with, do you think?'

I considered this. I was about to recommend *Great Expectations* or *David Copperfield* when I remembered we were approaching Christmas.

'*A Christmas Carol*,' I suggested. 'I think you'll enjoy that. Wait here a moment and I'll nip and get it.' I ran upstairs and quietly opened the bedroom door, though Noelle wasn't asleep. She was sitting up in bed, daydreaming. She'd brushed out her pin curls and it looked like she was wearing mascara, though none of us has any so she must have made do with some of Papa's boot polish.

'What are you up to?' she asked.

'I'm lending the German *A Christmas Carol*,' I explained.

'Let's not call him that, Queenie. He might be the enemy but he's not a Nazi. He's a good Catholic and he hates this war as much as we do. Please don't call him "the German". He's called Wolfgang,' my sister said, then she flushed, embarrassed at her outburst. 'Why are you lending him books, anyway?' she asked next.

I shrugged. 'Because he asked,' I replied, and I darted out of the room again, clutching the novel. As I shut the bedroom door, I glanced again at Noelle's face and saw it was no longer dreamy. Instead, I saw written across her beautiful features a feeling I'm not sure she'd ever experienced before. Jealousy. She didn't want me making friends with Wolfgang. Well, she has no reason to be jealous. Even if I weren't in love with Albert, there's no way I'd be interested in a German – whether he's a decent one or not; though I suppose it's understandable that some of the local girls are falling for these handsome strangers, with so few young men of our own remaining. I just hope Noelle sees sense and nips in the bud any feelings she may have for him – for all our sakes.

One last thing I must just report. From time to time, we get Germans coming into the salon – which quickly kills any conversation we might be enjoying. Not that many, as we're a long way out of town, but there are various soldiers and officers billeted around the St Ouen area, including – unfortunately – the Grim One. Yesterday, he came into the salon for the first time. Of course, nobody wanted to be the one to cut his hair, but Sabine scuttled out to the back before I had a chance and Odette suddenly had a pressing need to nip to Downer's, the bakery, so I was the only hairdresser available. Diane was the only other customer and she was reading the *Evening Post* while her curlers were in – we were doing her favourite: the Hollywood wave. She looks just like Veronica Lake, with her creamy skin and her long blonde hair.

The Grim One nodded to Diane and said 'Madam' in a courteous sort of way. She just blushed and hid behind the paper. Then he turned to me. He wasn't quite so polite with a lowly hairdresser like me.

'I vood like a short beck und sides, as I understand you call it. And make it qvick. I have no time to vaste.' He chose a seat and, having made a show of brushing some non-existent hair off the chair, he sat down on it and clasped his hands together in a bizarrely priestly sort of way. His skin looked all pale and waxy. I felt a bit queasy, stood there behind him with a pair of scissors in my hand. I forced myself to look him in the eye through the mirror and started to make a bit of conversation, but he cut me dead.

'Vas it not ze great leader of ze British Isles who, ven asked by his barber, "How vood you like your hair cut?" replied vith ze answer, "In silence." I sink I have at last found somezing in common vith him.'

I felt like sticking my tongue out at him then but I didn't. Instead, I carried out another small act of resistance. Right at the part of his greasy head that he'll never be able to see in a mirror, I shaved a circular patch! I took a gamble on the fact no one will dare point it out to him – perhaps they'll think he's going bald. I sincerely hope no one's bold enough to mention it, anyway. Oh, it did make me want to giggle. When I finished, I carefully avoided showing it to him and as soon as he'd gone – the ungrateful miser didn't leave a tip – I rushed to the back to tell Sabine and we didn't half have a good chuckle. Only a small win against the enemy, but a thrilling and satisfying one.

Chapter Fifteen

CANTERBURY, DECEMBER 2016

LIBERTY

Much as Libby adored Henry and her children, she'd come to the con-
clusion that she needed this break far more than her mother needed
Libby's help. She was sleeping like a baby for the first time in years and
this alone had reduced her anxiety no end.

Over breakfast, Tink quizzed her daughter on the argument with
Stella. 'You told me you'd fallen out and then Henry rang about Amy
and it all went completely out of my head. I'm such a dreadful flutter-
brain! What on earth happened?'

Libby refilled their cups with tea from the china pot. 'It's a long
story, Mum. I told Dad all about it last night. It's to do with the grudge
– the grudge between our families that you and Dad never told me
about.'

Tink looked shamefaced. 'Oh! Oh dear. Well . . . it never seemed
to be an issue between you and Stella, so we just let sleeping dogs lie.
Why on earth has it all come to the surface now?'

'You know that her mother Sybil died recently? Well, it seems that on her deathbed she finally told Stella all about the grudge and the reasons for it.'

'Oh, but I'm sure Stella will only have heard one side of the story. Alf will tell you what really happened, won't you, dear?'

'Lib's already asked me to. But then she'd only have another unreliable side of the story and why should she believe me? You can't always trust your old dad, you know.' Alf smiled across at Libby and continued spreading jam methodically on his toast. 'No, if Libby wants the truth, she's going to have to see the best evidence of it. I've lent her the journal. She's going to read it.'

'I'm going to make a start this morning,' Libby explained.

'Okay, my darling. Well, you're a quick reader at least. We're going to try to get to the supermarket. We'll be an hour or so. If we're not back by this afternoon, call a search party!'

Once her parents had left – after a couple of false starts, having forgotten first the carrier bags and then Tink's purse – Libby turned her phone to 'Silent', made herself a coffee and went through to the living room to settle down on the sofa with Queenie's journal, Coco and Chanel snuggled up beside her. With the fairy lights from the tree in the corner glinting and a light shower of snow falling outside, she felt rather peaceful. It was the perfect setting to get stuck into Queenie's journal. She'd just reached the bit about the poor slave worker Queenie had found in the road when her phone began to vibrate in her pocket. She growled inwardly.

'Hello?' she said, rather sharply.

'Libby, it's Henry. I'm afraid something shattering has happened.'

'What?'

'It's Liam.'

'What's happened?' Libby asked, jumping to her feet, her phone clamped to her ear. She felt ice cold with dread.

'He took some of those so-called legal highs. I think I've heard you and Stella refer to them as NPS or something?'

'New psychoactive substances, that's right. They can be lethal. Is he okay? Please tell me he's okay,' Libby begged.

'He had a seizure.'

'A seizure?' Libby fell back down onto the sofa with a thump.

'He's stable. He had a fit, frothing at the mouth – that sort of thing. The drugs were from a particularly dodgy batch, apparently. There's already been one death. I don't know if you remember? It was in the paper. We're lucky he didn't die.' Henry's voice, usually so strong and steady, sounded wobbly.

'Are you sure he's going to be okay? Where . . . where is he?' Libby asked, barely able to get her words out in her shocked panic.

'At the General Hospital. He's sedated at the moment but the doctors have said there won't be any lasting damage, thank the Lord.'

'But when did this happen? Surely not this morning?'

'At two o'clock this morning he had a seizure after leaving a nightclub. He was on his own but a patrolling police officer witnessed it and called for an ambulance, then went with Liam to A & E. I was contacted immediately, so I got there at about three. I'm sorry, I should have called sooner, but I didn't want to wake you in the night, with no way of getting home, and then the time has just vanished and I only remembered I hadn't called you ten minutes ago. I thought I should book you onto a flight before I called. It's this afternoon, three twenty-five. Will you be able to get to the airport in time?'

'Yes, I'm sure . . . Mum and Dad are out at the moment but they should be back soon. I'd better go and pack. I'll come straight to the hospital.'

'Okay. And Libby, don't beat yourself up about not being here. He's a grown man, not a baby. It's just Sod's Law this happens when, for once in your life, you've made a trip away.'

His words were kindly but Libby inevitably started to blame herself. Why was he taking drugs? Why hadn't she managed to stop him poisoning himself? Should she have done something, had him sent to rehab or something, back when he'd first told her about his occasional use? Why wasn't she there, right now, to make him better? Enough! She needed to stop thinking and start packing. She raced upstairs and started hurling clothes into her case as though she were a heroine in a film, the cats – who'd followed her up – helpfully jumping in and out of it. At the last minute, she remembered the journal was downstairs and ran down to get it, then stuffed it into her handbag. By the time her parents returned, she'd booked a taxi and was sitting on her case in the lobby.

'Glory be! What on earth's the matter?' asked Tink. Alf was following behind her with bags of groceries.

'It's Liam,' she explained. 'He took some dodgy drugs. He's had a seizure. He's okay; he's stable. But he's in hospital. I've booked a taxi to the station. It'll be here in a minute. I'm so sorry to have to leave like this . . .' Libby said, struggling not to cry and then failing miserably.

'Good heavens, don't be daft. Liam is your priority. Oh, my poor darling, come here and give me a hug,' said Tink, and she clasped Libby to her. When she let go, Libby looked up to see Alf proffering another handkerchief. It was navy with white dots on it. He dried Libby's tears with the square of linen and then curled her hand around it.

'Keep it,' he said, and Libby kept hold of that hanky the whole way through her journey to Gatwick, treating it like a comfort blanket, then wringing it between her hands as she sat on the plane and willed the pilot to jolly well get on with it when he started apologising for a short delay until take-off. Finally, the jet began to trundle along the runway and then up towards the clouds.

Jersey looked at its most alluring as the plane started to descend. The sun was about to set over St Ouen's Bay and the whole island was bathed in pink light. Everything glowed and shone: the green patchwork of potato fields soon to be planted with Jersey royals, the granite farm buildings, the reservoir, the high tide slapping over the sea wall, the fortifications up and down the sweep of the bay, built by those poor slave workers Libby was learning about in Queenie's journal. As Henry had told her, the English cold snap had completely missed the island – it looked more like spring than December, though apparently there were storms forecast and there was even a small chance the island would be hit by the snow that had recently covered the south-east.

Surveying it all from above as the plane landed, Libby breathed in and felt a wonderful, peaceful sense of coming home, despite the difficult circumstances. An hour later, having navigated the baggage hall, customs and the taxi rank, she arrived to find Liam in his hospital room. It was typically clinical and bland, with a pitiful tinsel arrangement at the foot of the bed – a painful reminder for patients and visitors that Christmas was just around the corner. Henry was nowhere to be seen but there, in a plastic chair beside Liam's bed, she saw a familiar shape, kitted out in a vast Peruvian-style poncho and reading a well-thumbed paperback. It was Stella.

Chapter Sixteen

Jersey, December 1941

Queenie's Journal

It's not long until Christmas now and I'm feeling quite optimistic, despite the fact that I *still* haven't heard from Albert. There have been no letters in or out – last month, a chap was sent to prison in France for trying to post letters to England for a number of locals, poor fellow. Thank goodness for the Red Cross, which is the only way anyone's able to get any news about loved ones. I still haven't received a message from Albert, though, and it's been ages since his parents last received anything from him.

Anyway, my cheery mood is down to the fact that last week we found out there are to be extra rations for Christmas week – the sugar ration has been doubled to six ounces and we'll receive two ounces of tea and the same of pipe tobacco, so Papa is thrilled. There will be chocolate for the children, too, so Albert's little sisters will be happy.

On top of that, the pantomime begins this afternoon – it's on for three days and will finish on Saturday (the 20th of December). It seems strange for the panto to be on before Christmas rather than afterwards, as is traditional, but Foxy thought it might boost morale to put it on beforehand – to try to induce a little bit of Christmas cheer. Odette has kindly given Sabine and me the time off to perform but, for most of the other actors, time off work isn't a problem – there's so little to sell nowadays for anyone who's a shopkeeper that they often shut early of an afternoon and many only open three days a week now, offering more of a trade or bartering system than anything else.

Once the pantomime is over, I'm not sure how I shall fill my spare time – I've never wished for time to go so quickly and never has it seemed to drag so slowly. It's just so isolating to be stuck here with no escape and with no communication with the outside world. I'm reading anything I can get my hands on, although there are increasingly slim pickings at the public library. In September last year, the Germans ordered the removal of any books they didn't approve of, many being burned – much to my horror – and the *Evening Post* has just reported a demand for all libraries to remove books with disparaging remarks about Germany before the end of the year. I pity the poor librarians!

The wireless is another important lifeline. There's not yet been the expected order to hand them in, so we're making the most of listening to the news broadcasts. There's a feeling of optimism about the war in Britain at the moment thanks to the new American allies, and there's less bombing going on – now that Hitler's fighting Russia, he needs to divert a lot of the *Luftwaffe* eastwards. Listening to tales of the blitz earlier this year and knowing Albert's up there fighting in the air terrifies me. I just hope he's safe. I don't even know if he's alive. I *feel* he is, but you never know, do you?

Golly, I've just realised the time. I must go or I'll be late for Diane, who's in charge of make-up as well as outfits (fortunately, the drama club had a decent stash of make-up before the occupation began). I'm pleased to say she does need to use quite a lot of cosmetics to make me sufficiently ugly for my role! It's lovely to play a villain. Before, I've always been the young damsel in distress or a chorus girl, so I'm relishing every moment of putting Cinderella (Sabine) in her place. Sabine is wonderfully forgiving! It's strange but I don't feel nervous; I never do.

It's like I become somebody else as soon as I walk on stage. I love it! I will write again later, once the show has finished . . .

It is late now. Papa opened a precious bottle of wine after the performance this afternoon to celebrate. It was such a success. Not down to me – though I adore acting, I'm also aware it's not something for which I have a natural talent – but down to the rest of the cast, Foxy and the amazing Diane. She really *is* talented. But the thing that really made it was the audience. As I stood on stage and cruelly ordered Cinders to dress my hair for the ball, it seemed to me as though the entire village was in attendance and the atmosphere was electric. The cheering, the boos, the applause! Everyone was in fits of laughter seeing Tommy in his part as the Fairy Godmother – I knew he'd have them in stitches. I'm so buoyed up now I don't know how I'll sleep.

But a sobering thought is that tomorrow, before work, I'm going to drop off a basket of food to Noelle's friend Sybil to help her family now they have an extra mouth to feed. Poor Rachel, hidden in the attic or wherever she might be. If I feel claustrophobic at not being able to leave the island or communicate with anyone from elsewhere, then I can only imagine how she must feel.

I am back in my own bed beside Noelle again now. I slept in the *cabinet* – the little room next to Mama and Papa's – while she was contagious (I could have slept in one of the attic rooms, which are larger, but Mama's convinced they're haunted) and she's snoring away as if she didn't have a care in the world. There's no doubt what – or should I say whom? – she's dreaming about. The doctor hasn't been round for a few days and his absence only seems to have intensified her feelings.

But enough dwelling on problems for now . . . I don't want to lose this rare glow of joy and excitement the pantomime has given me. I must savour the moment . . .

Chapter Seventeen

Jersey, December 2016

Liberty

'You're kidding me!' Libby whispered furiously, seeing Stella sitting there beside a sleeping Liam. He was in a side room, rather than a ward, so thankfully they had some privacy. 'For heaven's sake, the poor boy hasn't even woken up yet! Can't he be allowed to see his own mother before you start interrogating him?'

'Do you think I'm that evil?' Stella whispered back angrily. 'I'm not here in an official capacity! I'm here as Liam's godmother!'

'Oh!' Libby was taken aback. Of course, the rift between her and Stella didn't necessarily mean Stella would no longer be interested in Libby's family. She felt instantly ashamed for thinking so badly of her. 'I'm sorry . . .' she began, but Stella – normally so hard to offend – was clearly not ready to forgive Libby. For anything.

She gathered up her bag and the book she'd been reading. She looked tired and Libby realised she must have been there, with Liam and Henry, since the early hours of the morning. 'Now that his mother's back, there's clearly no room for a godmother. If I'm permitted visiting rights, please let me know.'

'Of course,' Libby said. 'I'm sorry, Stella. I'm just so worried. I'm not thinking straight. Please, come back and see him anytime.'

Stella stopped at the doorway and turned towards Libby. She looked her in the eye. 'I'm sorry,' she said, and Libby felt her heart swoop with hope. 'About Liam. I'll be back to visit later.'

Libby watched her leave, bobbles from her folksy shoulder bag trailing along the lino floor. Then she crept towards Liam's bed and perched on the side of it. He was tucked underneath starched white sheets and a peach-coloured blanket, his blond curls all ruffled, and he looked just as young and innocent as when she'd tucked him into bed as a child. His skin was pale and there was some fair stubble on his chin. His thick eyelashes lay heavily over his eyes and she wondered what he was dreaming about beneath those rapidly moving lids.

'Oh, Liam,' she said, tracing a finger lightly across his forehead. But he didn't stir. After a while, she moved to the bedside chair and watched the nice, non-judgemental nurses bustle in and out of the room. She was still wondering where Henry might be. Eventually he turned up, red in the face and panting.

'I went to meet you at the airport!' he said.

'Oh, I'm so sorry! I didn't think! I just hopped in a taxi. I imagined you'd be needed here. I hadn't realised Stella was standing in for me.'

Henry looked uncomfortable. 'Ah, yes. Look, you don't mind, do you? She was on duty and she heard what happened, so she came straight to the hospital. She's been a brick, she really has. But I know it's a bit awkward between you . . .'

'Well, it certainly was when I turned up and was shocked to see her. You should have warned me!'

'Yes, I should have. I'm sorry!' Henry said, hanging his head. Libby didn't have the heart to stay angry for long.

'Come here,' she said. 'Give me a hug. This isn't a day for petty arguments between any of us. This is about Liam.' Libby paused. 'What about Amy and Milo? What's happening with them? Are they okay?'

'Amy's been in to see Liam but I haven't said much to Milo – I made something up about a work crisis in the night. He's gone to stay with the Atkinsons. I wasn't sure how honest to be.'

'Completely, I think. There couldn't be a better deterrent for him, to see his brother lying here like this. I've been watching him. Do you remember when he and Amy were kids and they used to stay awake whenever we went out to dinner so they could pretend to be asleep when we got home and checked on them?'

Henry laughed. 'I'd forgotten that. They used to get into the same bed and feign sleep so that we'd say they looked sweet!'

'We always fell for it. "Don't they look adorable?" we used to say, and then they'd burst out laughing, unable to keep up the pretence but so proud of themselves for managing to fool us. I was looking at him just now and remembering that – wondering if, right now, he's pretending to be asleep so he doesn't have to deal with the fallout from all of this.'

Henry turned to look at his son. 'No, he's definitely asleep. If he was awake, he'd argue that it was all Amy's idea.'

'Yes,' Libby smiled. 'You're right. He would.'

Henry paused, then, very quietly, he said, 'Did you know, Libby? Did you know that he takes drugs?'

Libby's eyes filled with tears. She nodded. 'Please don't be cross that I didn't tell you. I know more than anyone the devastating effects drugs have on users and their families, but I just thought it was a passing fad. You know what he's like. A flash in the pan . . .'

'We don't talk enough. We don't communicate. I'm not cross with you, Libby. It's my fault. My job – it comes before everything. It always has done. And I'm sorry,' he said, reaching for Libby's hand. 'Things are going to be different now.'

Libby took Henry's hand and kissed it. 'A second chance. For all of us.'

Chapter Eighteen

JERSEY, DECEMBER 1941

QUEENIE'S JOURNAL

It's the 19th of December today, and it's strange as it's not actually that cold. Just as well, really, given the fuel restrictions. It's the only time I've ever been pleased not to have a white Christmas.

I went on a couple of visits before work this morning. I took a heavy basket round to Mrs Lucas, breathing in great gusts of sea air as I walked. The tide was high and the air had a freshness to it that I only wished I could bottle.

Mama said the basket just had homemade bread in it but I thought it was too weighty for that and when I got there Mrs Lucas unpacked it and squealed with delight when she saw there was some pork underneath the bread. Papa has obviously stuck to his promise of a Christmas pig and is surreptitiously sharing the perks of being a farmer with our neighbour and her secret house guest. The pieces were neatly dealt with, too – Papa's deft with a knife.

Mrs Lucas called to Oleg, who emerged from the larder, having obviously hidden in there when I'd knocked on the door, and he rushed over to give me a hug and thank me. He's looking so much better than he did. Even his hair is starting to grow back. Mrs Lucas told me she's giving Oleg English lessons and that he's a very keen student. I can imagine that, with his bright and intelligent-looking eyes.

After that, I nipped home to pick up another basket – this one lighter – to take to Sybil's family up at Violet's school. Mama came with me on this visit, her silver hair protected from the wind by a headscarf, and we took turns carrying it along Route des Havres and up Mont du Valet, squawking seagulls circling us as we climbed. I knew what was in this one – lots of veggies, some more bread, jam and a few eggs. When we got there, Sybil's mother, Violet, hugged us gratefully, but she looked strained.

'How's Rachel?' I whispered.

'She's okay. She's up in the attics. Come and see her quickly – she'll be glad of a bit of company. I'm afraid I must get to class in a minute. Today's the last day of term. Oh, here's Sybil,' she said, seeing her daughter striding along the hallway. 'She'll take you up. A warning, though, Sybil's very cross!'

'What's the matter?' I asked, seeing Sybil's face. She was dressed in one of her boiler suits and, as usual, her hair was tied up in a turban.

'Had my bicycle stolen, that's what!' she replied. 'Went into town yesterday and parked it outside Le Marquand's and when I came out I saw some woman riding off on it! I tried to chase her down – I was shouting and screaming like a madwoman – but she got away! Only good thing was that the rear tyre went last week and I replaced it with a bit of hose – not comfortable for the wretched thief at least!'

Mama tutted. 'It's happening more and more nowadays. Stealing bicycles, snitching on your neighbours . . . A sad sign of the times.'

'I'm furious about it . . . And there's no chance of finding one to replace it, is there? How am I going to get about now?'

'You can borrow mine,' I told her. 'Just as long as I'm not using it. Or Noelle's got one and she doesn't go out and about as much as me.'

Sybil brightened. 'Oh, thank you! You're an angel,' she said, and Mama gave me a smile of approval.

We passed Mary Jane's lovely old mum, Ivy, who was mopping the floor, and followed Sybil up the back stairs. We waited while she gently knocked on the door. Rachel opened it and Sybil disappeared off, leaving us to it. Rachel didn't half look a fright – so pale and fragile and afraid. We both gave her a hug and she implored us to sit down, which we did. Mama made lots of comforting clucking noises and told Rachel she must try to keep her strength up.

'Make sure you keep your muscles working, my love. Take a turn around the attics three times a day, won't you?'

'I do nothing else,' Rachel replied. 'If I keep moving, I don't think quite so much.'

'What's it like?' I asked. 'Being up here all day and all night?'

'Better than the alternative.' Rachel's dark eyes were full of sorrow and, even safely hidden away up there, she whispered. I think the worst thing about seeing Rachel up in that attic was realising that all this business has robbed her of her wonderful sense of humour. 'Anyway,' she continued, 'I wouldn't trust myself to walk past any of those Nazis on the street. I would spit at them or something terrible and I'd soon find myself packed off to . . .'

She couldn't even say it but we knew what she was talking about. A concentration camp. The very words strike horror in us all, but for Rachel the prospect is very real.

'Has there been a notice in the paper about me?' she asked. 'I keep asking my lovely hosts and they tell me no but I don't know if they're just being kind.'

I shook my head. 'Not yet,' I told her, but this afternoon I picked up my copy of the *Evening Post* after I finished at the salon and before the show, and there – on page four – I saw it. It sent a jolt of terror through me.

NOTICE

The German authorities are looking for Miss Rachel
Weider (see photograph), typist, of Polish national-
ity, 18 years of age, formerly residing at 14a Rose
Street, St Peter. She has been missing from her
residence since 5th December, 1941, and has
evaded the German authorities. Any person who
knows the whereabouts of Miss Weider is requested to get in touch with Feldkommandantur 515,
who will treat any information with the strictest of
confidence. Anyone concealing Miss Weider or
aiding her in any other manner makes himself liable to punishment.

DIE FELDKOMMANDANTUR
Jersey, 19.12.1941

I had to put it out of my mind when I arrived at the parish hall
for our second performance, though. No use being distracted when
there's a big crowd needing entertaining. If anything, this afternoon's
was an even better reception than the first one, with Mama shocking
everyone with her loud wolf whistles – bless her, she always comes to
every single show I appear in. I spotted the Grim One in the audience,
frowning at Mama.

I can't wait for tomorrow – the final performance is always my
favourite – and it's Noelle's birthday, too, so if she's feeling strong
enough, she's going to come along and watch. I really hope she does.
In fact, I'm almost certain she will, as Wolfgang visited today and
told her he's going to be there. There can't be a better incentive for
her than that.

Chapter Nineteen

Jersey, December 2016

Liberty

'Mum,' Liam croaked eventually, seeing Libby by his side. It was late, now, almost ten and Henry had gone home to get some sleep.

'How are you feeling?' Libby asked immediately.

'Stupid, mainly. And tired. But okay. Mum, I'm so, so sorry.'

'I'm just ecstatic you're alive! But, Liam, what possessed you to take a legal high? You know I warned you about those!'

'Don't ask me. I wasn't thinking straight last night. I'd had a bad day at work on Friday, had too much to drink all weekend . . . met the wrong person in the wrong place . . .'

'Please, Liam, just promise me you won't touch anything like that ever again.'

'I promise,' said Liam. 'I feel like a prize idiot. I don't exactly relish the idea of repeating this experience.' Then, in a tiny voice, he added, 'And I was so scared, Mum. I honestly thought I was going to die.'

Liam grasped Libby's hand and she squeezed her eyes shut. 'Well, thank goodness you didn't.' She felt short of breath just thinking about it. 'Look, I'm in dire need of a coffee,' she said, needing to compose herself. 'I'm just going to get one from the machine down the corridor. Do you want anything? Are you allowed anything?'

'No, I don't think so. Just water for now.'

When Libby reached the door, Liam's voice stopped her. 'Mum!'

'Yes, darling?' she said, turning round.

'Thanks for being you – for not giving me a lecture or disowning me or anything . . . For just showing me love.' Libby gave him a watery smile but didn't cry until she'd made it down the corridor. Once she'd got herself together, she bought herself one of the super-heated coffees from the machine and made her way back to Liam's room.

She was about to open the door when she realised she'd spilt some of her coffee on the floor. 'Damn!' she said to herself. She looked around and spotted a paper towel dispenser on the wall, so she grabbed a few sheets and started mopping up. It was only then, on her knees outside Liam's room, that she realised she could hear voices from inside. She put her ear to the door.

'Can you remember anything about the guy? What he was wearing, any mannerisms, anything? Even the smallest bit of information could be helpful.'

Libby felt the blood rise to her cheeks and her knees begin to tremble. *Do you think I'm that evil?* Stella had said when Libby accused her of waiting by Liam's bedside to interrogate him about his dealer. And she was back, right now, doing exactly that. Libby pushed the door open with such force she nearly knocked out a nurse who'd been doing Liam's obs. For a second, Libby was confused. Had Liam just been talking to the nurse? But then she saw Stella with her chair pulled up close to Liam's bed, looking guiltily at Libby.

'Stella, could I speak to you for a moment?' Libby asked in a dangerously calm voice.

'Of course . . . I . . .' Stella faltered. She followed behind Libby's upright back along the corridor to the coffee machine.

Libby turned towards her. 'How *dare* you? You promised me you were here as a godmother, not a detective! How could you betray my trust like that? Here's you de-friending me over some grudge that has nothing whatsoever to do with us as individuals and then you go and do something like this. It's unforgivable!'

Libby, unused to speaking her mind, was shaking.

'I'm sorry, I really am,' Stella replied. 'But Libby, you don't understand. There's this batch of NPS on the street at the moment that's completely lethal. If Liam could just tell me who it was that sold it to him, he could save lives . . .'

'You're not sorry at all! Listen to you, Stella, putting your job before anything or anyone else, as always. No wonder Ben had enough of it! Poor man always played second fiddle to your job!'

Libby spoke quickly, immediately regretting her stinging words. Stella looked at Libby as if she'd been physically slapped. 'I am sorry, Libby, actually. But it just so happens I care about my job, just like Henry cares about his. You're the one with the problem, Libby, can't you see that? So insecure that you can't handle either of us devoting ourselves to our work for fear we might not give you the attention you crave. Think about that, why don't you!'

Stella was off, her poncho whooshing up into the air as she hurried towards the lift, leaving Libby bobbing about in the wreckage of their friendship, lost at sea and hoping desperately for a lifeline.

It arrived a moment later in the form of Henry. 'I couldn't sleep,' he said, rushing towards Libby to embrace her. 'Hey, what's up?' he asked, seeing her face.

'Henry, the rift between Stella and me just got a whole lot worse. She said I'm the one with the problem, not you. About your job. That I'm an attention-seeker and that's why I can't handle you giving your all to your vocation.'

'Oh, hogwash!' Henry comforted. 'I've never known anyone less attention-seeking than you. I'm absolutely the one with the problem,

Libby. She'll have just been speaking heatedly in the moment. I expect you pressed one of her buttons.'

Libby thought about her words to Stella – the cutting remark about her ex, Ben. Stella had never got over Ben leaving her. Though she'd spoken the truth – he couldn't handle Stella's commitment to her job – it had been unfair of Libby to press on such a raw nerve. And although her protectiveness of Liam was still at the forefront of her mind, she realised that Stella's motives in talking to him were in fact very noble.

Libby and Henry walked together into Liam's room.

'Liam,' Libby said, grasping his hand. 'Can you remember anything about the dealer? Think about it. It's so important. You've got a chance here to prevent this happening to someone else.'

Liam rubbed his eyes, groaning. 'Look, I've told Stella already, I can't remember anything . . . I was drunk, then out of it, then fitting . . .' He closed his eyes. 'Though . . . there was just one thing.'

'Yes?' Libby asked.

'He had a birthmark. I remember that. I can't remember anything else. Just this strawberry mark on his cheek, beneath his left eye, like a teardrop.'

'Stella said it didn't matter how small, it could be useful,' Libby said. 'I'll be back in a minute.'

She dashed back along the corridor and dialled Stella's number but she was obviously screening and the call went straight to voicemail.

'Stella, I have something. Liam's remembered something about the dealer. Stella, call me.'

Chapter Twenty

Queenie's journal

I am shaking, which is why my writing is a little wobbly. Only half an hour until the curtain goes up on our last performance. I thought I'd have longer to get this down but I'd better be quick. Sabine and I have done something very silly. Why we chose to do it on the morning of our final performance I'm not sure. I suppose we didn't think too hard about the consequences . . .

It's a Saturday and we always start work early, as it's our busiest day. As soon as I'd given Noelle her birthday present (a knitted scarf – I made it by unravelling an old jumper and it looks lovely as a scarf), I gave her a big kiss and went on my way. I usually meet Sabine at the salon but I was cycling up Mont Pinel when she came freewheeling down the hill towards me and screeching to a halt. She was full of beans.

'What are you so happy about?' I asked, puffed out from the steep hill.

'Look!' she said, and she delved inside her satchel and brought out a couple of large lumps of white chalk.

'Where on earth did you get those from?' I was surprised, as every tiny commodity is hard to come by these days.

'Never you mind about that. The important thing is what we're going to do with them,' Sabine said with a cheeky smile.

'What are you going on about?' I asked her. 'Come on, we haven't got time for you being cryptic. We've got customers in twenty minutes!'

'You know, for somebody so damn clever, you can be pretty slow sometimes! You remember that BBC broadcast all about how occupied Europe could do its bit by putting up sneaky "V for Victory" signs? Well, my cousin Jimmy said he and his mates have been doing it in town. I thought we should do our bit for St Ouen! What d'you reckon?' Sabine's eyes were dark and dancing with mischief. It was contagious.

'Go on, then,' I agreed. 'But where?'

'On the road here, we'll chalk a great big "V" on it. No one'll be about this time of day and it won't take us five minutes. You keep lookout while I make a start!'

Sabine was right. It was quiet as anything, with just a couple of nosy gulls swooping down to see what we were up to. Sabine started chalking while I kept an eye on the road so I could warn her if I saw anyone. Only trouble was, we'd both forgotten the tiny lane that creeps up to the main road, only fifty yards away – Rue de Mahaut.

'Almost done. Just help me with this last bit!' Sabine shouted to me and I took one of the lumps of chalk. We finished the 'V' with a flourish, just as we heard a barked order behind us.

'Stop right zere!' a man shouted. We both froze. We heard heavy-booted footsteps march towards us. My legs had turned to jelly. 'Turn around!' the voice ordered.

We did. And I could have thrown up then and there when I saw who it was. The Grim One.

'Vot do you sink you are doing?' he asked, in a quieter, more sinister voice.

'It was all my fault,' Sabine confessed immediately. 'Please let my friend off. It was all my idea. A stupid prank, really. Nothing more than that.' Sabine was blinking back tears.

'Identity cards,' the Grim One said next, holding out his hand. We produced them with quivering hands. He took a few moments to study them. You could tell he was enjoying the power he had over us.

'You vill be in serious trouble for zis most serious of crimes – zis is an anti-German demonstration and vill not be tolerated. I sink I know you, do I not?' he asked Sabine, lifting her chin up. Then he turned to me. 'And you, too!'

'We're in the village pantomime,' Sabine answered. 'You might have seen us in that?' she asked, her voice trembling.

'Ah, yes. Hmm. Vell, I vill not be responsible for dampening ze island's morale. I vill be attending the show again tonight and you vill report to me afterwards. I vill vait for you directly outside ze parish hall. Between now and zen, I suggest you explain your conduct to your families. You vill almost certainly be looking at a prison sentence.' At this he gave us a villainous smile and turned on his heel, leaving us standing in the road, quaking with fear.

Sabine was ever so apologetic but I assured her I could easily have told her not to be so daft instead of joining in with her idea, though I was thinking about those young girls who went to prison for three days just for spitting cherry stones at some soldiers, and I dreaded to think what we'd be looking at.

Somehow we got through our morning customers. Then, at lunchtime, Sabine went off to tell Odette and I cycled home to tell Papa and Mama. Papa was furious – more so with the Germans than me but nonetheless he gave me a good telling-off. For getting caught more than the act itself, mind you. Mama could see what a state I was in and was doing her best to hide her own worry. She made me a nice cup of proper tea she'd squirrelled away for emergencies.

'Now, don't you be worrying about this all through the show. Best thing you can do for yourself and your island is to go and perform your little socks off now. Come on, my love, I'll walk with you up to the parish hall so you've some company. You need to get there for the final run-through before the last performance. Papa will join us later. And he's going to bring Noelle, too. She's so excited. You need to put on a good show for her or she won't understand what I've been raving about!'

I'm now up at the hall and it's chaos, as it always is before the show. But there's a slightly odd and uneasy atmosphere. A little bit tense. I thought this might have been down to my own jangled nerves but I've just witnessed something unsettling. I was going to find Diane in the little room at the back so she could do my make-up for me but when I made my way down the darkened corridor, I heard raised voices. I peeped round the corner into the room and saw my nemesis, the Grim One, squared up to Diane in the midst of an angry exchange. I retreated, sneaking behind the piano in the corridor before either of them noticed me, but still with a view of the set-to. I couldn't believe my eyes when I saw Diane slap the Grim One round the face! He shouted something in German before striding out of the room and down the corridor. Poor Diane was in tears.

'What happened? Are you all right?' I asked her, but she just blew her nose and told me it was nothing. As soon as she'd finished with my make-up and she'd moved on to Sabine's, I made a beeline for my journal so I could get everything down. If the Grim One's threatening Sabine and me with prison for chalking the road, goodness knows what Diane's in for after slapping him across the face.

The pantomime's about to start, so I must sign off for now. I know it's risky to have brought the diary with me this afternoon, but I don't know if Sabine and I will be whisked away by the Grim One after the show and I want to be able to keep a record of whatever happens next. I've got a decent inside pocket in my coat, so I can hide it away in there.

Foxy's just found me. 'You ready?' he asked. I smiled at him, then gave him my Ugly Sister stare – already in character – which made him laugh. 'Five minutes till show time!' he told me, racing off in a dramatic fluster.

I can't help wondering if this will be my last performance ever.

Chapter Twenty-One

Jersey, December 2016

Liberty

'Mum, I can definitely go home today, the doctor just told me!' Liam said, grinning from ear to ear. Libby had gone home for a couple of hours' rest and it was now nine in the morning on Tuesday. She'd left Henry at home organising for a locum to take the school carol concert in the afternoon, so he could spend some time with Libby and Liam. Libby couldn't remember the last time Henry had used a locum and she knew he was sticking to his word about trying to achieve a better work–life balance.

'Oh, that's wonderful news! You will come home to the Vicarage, darling, won't you? I can't bear the thought of you being alone in your flat.'

'Er, actually, I need to talk to you about that. You know I said I'd had a bad day at work on the Friday before this all happened? Well, it's because I lost my job, Mum. That was the reason for my weekend binge. I'm going to have to let the flat go unless I find another job straight away. Could I move back home for a bit? Just until I get myself sorted out?'

'Of course you can. But what happened? At the bank?'

'There was this girl I met at a club a couple of months ago. A French girl. She lives in Paris. We started emailing each other jokey stuff. Only some of it was a bit explicit. The IT guys did some kind of sweep of the system and found the emails. I was asked to leave immediately.'

Libby closed her eyes. First Milo and his sexting and now Liam with his explicit emails. What was wrong with her children? She clenched her jaw in an effort not to let rip her thoughts on the matter. After all, Liam needed treating with kid gloves after everything that had happened.

'I'm sorry, Mum,' Liam said.

'You're saying that a lot at the moment,' Libby replied. 'I'll tell you what. You're welcome to come back home but there are some house rules. No drugs. No sexting. And no explicit emails. Okay?'

'Sure,' Liam agreed sheepishly. 'What's the thing with the sexting?'

'I'll tell you later. It's a whole other story involving your brother.'

Liam's blue eyes widened. 'Poor Mum. We're all giving you grief at the moment.'

'There's one other thing I need you to do,' Libby pressed on. 'What you told me about the dealer. When Stella finally gets back in touch with me, I need you to speak to her – to give a statement if necessary. I can't bear for this to happen to another family.'

Liam nodded, then looked towards the door. Stella pushed it open tentatively. She couldn't meet Libby's eyes but she slowly walked towards Liam.

'You've got something for me?' she asked, getting straight to the point.

'He had a birthmark – the dealer. That's all I can remember.'

Stella looked pensive. 'What sort of birthmark?'

'A strawberry-coloured one on his cheek. I noticed it because it was shaped like a teardrop. It made him look sad.'

'Pierrot,' Stella breathed.

'Is it helpful?' Libby asked.

'More than you know,' Stella replied.

On Wednesday, with Liam happily ensconced in front of Netflix with an array of soft drinks and snacks, Libby returned to work, having cancelled the remainder of her holiday and booked the period between Christmas and New Year off instead. On her walk from the car park, noticing the aerial display of festive lights and the shop windows rammed with goods to tempt Christmas shoppers and sparkly dresses to entice partygoers, Libby realised it was 21 December and she still hadn't embarked on any of her preparations for the celebrations ahead. With Liam safely home and Amy and Milo taking a break from driving her daft, she needed to get on with it.

In her lunch hour she narrowly avoided sharing the lift with Glenda, then burst out of the front doors onto King Street, relishing the fresh air like a convict just released from prison. She pulled her belted coat around her and shrank into her scarf: it had suddenly cooled down considerably, with the wind getting up as well. She battled the gusty streets, making her way to the central market where, within the red iron gates, she found her favourite butcher's – *Le Brun & Sons*.

'Afternoon, my love,' said the butcher. 'Haven't seen you for a while. What can I do for you?'

'I know, Frank, and I've left it dreadfully late, but can I order my turkey?'

The man sucked his teeth. 'Ooh, you are cutting it fine. Lucky I ordered one for you! I know you get one from me every year. Couldn't see why this year would be different. You come back on Christmas Eve to pick it up!' The chap grinned, delighted at his shrewd foresight.

'That's amazing!' Libby smiled. 'You've restored my faith in humanity!'

'Just doing my job. Anything else while you're here?'

'A dozen of those nice local sausages please,' Libby requested, then handed over some cash and took the neatly wrapped package from her friendly butcher.

'Now, to Blossoms . . .' Libby said to herself as she passed the central fountain and wended her way to the smallest of the flower stalls. There wasn't so much choice but she liked the lady, who spent her spare moments with her nose in the *Telegraph* crossword. She clapped her mittened hands together when she saw Libby.

'Got brisk all of a sudden, hasn't it? The bookies have stopped taking bets on a white Christmas.'

'No way! I think I was a toddler the last time we had one of those. They don't really think it's going to snow, do they?'

'It's all anyone's talking about. Storms, too. Hopefully, everyone'll get where they need to be for Christmas before the weather sets in.'

'Yes, let's hope so. Everyone will be panic buying.'

'As long as that includes flowers, I don't mind!'

'I was wondering if you could deliver a nice arrangement on Christmas Eve – something festive for the dining table?'

'Of course, with a candle as the centrepiece?'

Libby thought for a moment. 'Yes, that would be lovely. And could you add one of those lovely wreaths for the door as well?' she asked, pointing to a pretty one made largely of pine cones and holly berries.

'Certainly can. Mistletoe, too?'

'Of course! Yes please. How about a tree? Do you have any?'

'These are all spoken for, I'm afraid, but you're in L'Etacq, aren't you? I know Didier's got a few left up at his lovely farm shop.'

'Good idea, I'll go there straight from work. Everyone gets their trees so early nowadays, don't they?'

'Well, it is the twenty-first today. Only a few days till Christmas!'

Libby started to feel rather festive. She made her way through the market, past Red Triangle Stores with its charming array of goods on display, from suitcases to plant pots to children's toys. Then across the road to the fish market on Beresford Street, where she bought a side of smoked salmon, hoping it would fit in the office fridge so she could keep it fresh until home time. With the salmon under her arm, she started to head back to the office but was lured into one of the department stores when she caught sight of the luxurious arrangements of toiletries and perfumes and make-up, thinking of getting a few extras for Amy, whose main gift she'd bought in Canterbury (a cream cashmere cardigan from The White Company). She was trying to remember which make-up brand Amy preferred when her favourite festive song started to play – 'Driving Home for Christmas'. She began to sing along, then smiled as she heard someone joining in behind her. Libby turned around to see Amy standing there, carrying a vast amount of expensive-looking carrier bags.

'Amy! Our favourite Christmas song!'

'I know, I came in through the doors and couldn't believe it when I saw you there singing along! I'd forgotten for a moment that you're back in Jersey! I just ducked out for an hour to get my Christmas shopping done. Actually, I'm glad I bumped into you. Could I ask a huge favour?'

Oh, here we go, thought Libby. 'Yeeess?'

'I'm about to get embroiled in this awful case at work and I'm not going to get a moment to breathe now until Christmas. Do you think you could take these bags with you and wrap everything for me? I'll text to tell you whose is whose so you can label them.' She started to pile the bags onto Libby's arms without waiting for her mother to agree to the request.

'All these? Are they just for the family?'

'Yes, and Stella. I'll wrap the ones for Jonty at some point, no idea when. I've ordered them online. Oh, hang on, give me that bag back, that's got yours in! Can't have you wrapping your own present!'

'No,' Libby replied faintly. By now she resembled a heavily burdened donkey.

Amy looked at her watch and gasped. 'Oh, gosh! Look at the time! I must dash. Thanks so much, Mum! I'll see you on Christmas Eve. Jonty's spending the evening with his parents but he'll join us on Christmas Day. I'll be with you about six. Byeee!' she called, heading off towards work without a backwards glance.

Libby trudged back to the office, having decided to forego the extra presents for Amy, and bumped straight into Glenda.

'Ooh, been shopping?' she remarked, stating the obvious.

'Yes, that's right,' Libby replied with a strained smile.

She'd just returned from wedging the salmon into the fridge when Farty found her. 'Ah, there you are, Libby. Glad you're back. We've got a rotten old case coming in this afternoon. We're dealing with the US, so I'm afraid I might need you to stay late over the next couple of days. You know – time difference and all that. You don't mind, do you?'

'Of course not,' Libby replied, though her heart began to race with panic. She'd have to ask Henry to pick up the tree. Her phone beeped – a text from Amy detailing the recipients of her gifts. Seized by an overwhelming sense of rebellion, Libby deleted it. She'd end up having to ask Amy to send it again but, for one fleeting moment, it felt intensely satisfying.

Chapter Twenty-Two

Jersey, December 1941

Queenie's journal

My hands were shaking when I wrote my journal this afternoon, but that was nothing compared with how they are now. But I must write – I need to get the events clear in my own mind before I decide what to do.

The final show went well, at least. The strange atmosphere seemed to evaporate as soon as the curtains drew up and the audience was wonderful: rowdy and loud and exactly what you want at a panto. I forgot a few of my lines but it didn't matter – I just made something up and it all worked perfectly well. Tommy was the star of the show and received a standing ovation. He tried to look like he couldn't have cared less but I could see his eyes twinkling with pride.

At the start of the show, when I'd made my appearance but before my speaking part, I had a good look round the crowd and spotted lots of familiar faces, including Mama and Papa and, I was thrilled to see, Noelle. Wolfgang was there, too, though obviously he wasn't sitting anywhere near my family. He was with a couple of German officers I didn't recognise. I was pleased the Grim One didn't seem to be there, though halfway through the performance I spotted him in the wings, whispering urgently to poor Diane. Clearly he couldn't keep away from her. Heaven only knows what's happening with him and Mary Jane – she didn't seem to be in the audience, as far as I could see.

When it was all over, the whole cast was absolutely on cloud nine. Diane left early – a headache after all the excitement – but the rest of us hung about while Tommy nipped to his house just along the road to get a bottle of brandy he'd managed to buy on the black market. We were starting to think he'd had second thoughts about sharing his booze but he blundered back eventually, clutching the bottle, panting and scarlet-faced. He'd obviously had a little glug en route but he handed it round generously. Sabine and I had a few good gulps each for Dutch courage, dreading our rendezvous with the Grim One. Mama found me mid-swig.

'Queenie, my love! What a wonderful job you did! I know you don't think you've a talent for acting but I disagree. Proud as punch, I was! Now, how are you feeling?'

'Nervous,' I admitted.

'Well, try not to be. There's no sign of that nasty officer, so I think he's letting you off the hook – for today, anyway. Will you be okay getting home on your own? Papa wants to get back and tell Mrs Lucas all about the show. She really wanted to come but she doesn't like to leave Oleg on his own,' she added with a whisper.

'Of course, I'll be fine. Oh, what a relief about the Grim One! Are you sure he's not around?'

'Positive. I've checked everywhere. Foxy says he left early.'

'You head off then, Mama. I'll be back in time for supper.'

Mama kissed my forehead. 'Take care, don't be too long.'

It wasn't that long afterwards that I said my farewells to Sabine – who was equally relieved – and the rest of the cast, and started to make my way home. I thought I'd take a shortcut only the locals know about. You have to put up with a few bramble scratches but it's a lot quicker and you can avoid any patrols. I was only a couple of minutes along the brambly path, dusk turning to darkness, when, dear me, I got the shock of my life.

There, curled up right in front of me on the path, was a body! And it wasn't moving. I nearly screamed. I wanted to run, instantly, but I steeled myself – I had to check if the man was alive, just in case he needed help. The figure was on his side, clutching himself, and it was only as I peered over and grabbed his wrist to check his pulse that I saw a long scar across his face, shimmering like mother-of-pearl in the twilight.

The Grim One! And he had no pulse. His arm felt stickily wet and as I pulled him towards me, trying to work out what had happened, I saw in the gloom his dark blood, now on my hands, and a knife. A great big butcher's knife, sticking out of his chest.

'Oh my goodness, oh my goodness,' I kept repeating to myself. His eyes looked glassy, like a fish, and his features had not been softened by death. What was I to do? Run back to the parish hall to tell someone? But there was nothing anyone could do to help him now, so I did what my instinct told me to. I let go of the body and I ran, as fast as I could – not back to the parish hall, but all the way home, where I scrubbed my hands until they were red raw. Somehow I got through Noelle's birthday supper, though I could barely eat – I had to feign a tummy upset – and now I'm upstairs on the bed writing this. I can hear Noelle playing the piano downstairs, entertaining Papa and Mama. The thunderous sonatas echo my thumping heart.

I must admit to conflicting feelings about the Grim One's death. I can't think of a person more deserving of his fate and yet perhaps he has a family somewhere who, despite everything, will miss him. As well, the responsibility of finding the Grim One's body is weighing heavily on me. I know I should report it, but if I do, I'll inevitably become a suspect, and we all know the Germans don't play a fair game. And, of course, it doesn't look good that I'm the one who found him dead on the very day he was going to arrest me for an anti-German demonstration.

I only hope he didn't tell any of his colleagues he'd caught Sabine and me chalking the 'V' sign on the road this morning. If he did, it won't be long until there's a knock at the door for both of us.

But if I'm spared that dreaded knock (oh, what a relief that would be!), then I don't think I have any option but to keep quiet. I won't be able to tell a soul; not even Sabine or Noelle.

That doesn't mean, however, that I won't be able to carry out my very own murder investigation . . . After all, I know it wasn't *me* who killed the Grim One, which leaves me desperate to know . . . who on earth *did*?

PART TWO

'A MAN CANNOT BE TOO CAREFUL IN HIS
CHOICE OF ENEMIES.'

From *The Picture of Dorian Gray*
By Oscar Wilde

Chapter Twenty-Three

LIBERTY

The following day, Libby's alarm clock woke her at six o'clock. It felt like the middle of the night – dark and freezing cold, the windows rattling in the wind. She could hear the roar of the incoming tide in the distance.

From the moment she got out of bed, leaving Henry slumbering, she realised it was going to be one of those days. They'd run out of milk so she had to drink her morning tea black, the bread was mouldy and she couldn't think for the life of her when she'd manage to fit in a dash for the essentials, let alone the big Christmas shop that would somehow have to be squeezed in during the next day or two. She contemplated giving the job to Henry, who at least worked from home, even if it was his busiest time of year, but she knew he'd forget vital items and so she resolved to get the main shopping done herself the following day – the twenty-third – after work. She started to make a list but none of the blasted pens in the kitchen were working and she felt her stress level rising by the minute, which was only exacerbated when Milo refused to get up, meaning he missed his bus to school.

'I'll take him,' Henry offered, appearing blearily in the kitchen, and Libby blew him a kiss of gratitude.

It was only on the drive into work, as she watched the enormous tide belching waves over the sea wall onto Victoria Avenue, soaking miserable commuter cyclists, that she realised why she was feeling particularly testy. It was her and Stella's franniversary – 22 December – the day when, had they not had their falling-out, they'd have been learning how to make Jersey Wonders as soon as the tide started to go out. Libby was well into Queenie's journal now, trying to read a little each night before her eyelids became too heavy and she sank into sleep, and she still had absolutely no idea what it was her grandparents could have done to Stella's family that was so terrible. Granny Noelle and Grandpa John were good, kind people who'd sadly died in their seventies, shortly before Noelle's sister Queenie and her husband, who were equally lovely. They'd all been far too young to leave this world. Remembering her grandparents as kindly figures who'd bought her sweets as a child and given invaluable advice to her as a young adult, she found it hard to imagine what they might have done that had been so catastrophic.

And Libby was beginning to wonder whether, even if the journal could throw light on the original reason for their row, she and Stella would ever be able to put behind them the words they had exchanged since. The whole thing was a mess. She sighed as she pulled into the car park and prowled about, looking for a space. It was only seven in the morning but Jersey workers were notorious early birds. She saw a red Fiesta about to reverse out of a space and waited patiently, indicating. She was about to manoeuvre into the space when an enormous great Range Rover came out of nowhere and wedged itself into the space she'd been waiting for.

Entirely out of character, Libby pressed on her horn belligerently. An aggressive-looking man with a red face opened the driver's door and slammed it behind him. He glared at Libby, then stormed off. Libby wound down her window. 'How very dare you!' she shouted out, but the man was gone.

The morning at work was heavy going but she managed to escape for an hour at lunchtime, heading for her favourite cafe: a lovely little place slightly off the beaten track. She ordered an egg sandwich and a mug of tea and settled down on a sofa in the hope of finishing Queenie's journal. She'd just got to the bit about the murder when she realised someone was saying her name.

'Stella!' she said, taken aback. 'How did you know I'd be here?'

'I know it's one of your favourite lunchtime haunts. I won't stay long. I just wanted to let you know what happened after Liam spoke to me on Tuesday – about the dealer,' she added with a whisper, looking around to make sure no one was eavesdropping.

'Sit down! Do you want a drink or anything?'

'No, I'm fine,' Stella replied, smoothing down her long skirt. Libby saw she was wearing her Birkenstocks, her poor toes looking pale and cold. She wanted to smile and joke about it but Stella's face was serious. 'I wanted to say thank you. As soon as Liam gave me the description, I knew exactly who the dealer was. Let's just say he's renowned. There was a raid at his flat early yesterday morning and he's been arrested. A huge amount of NPS was seized. He's looking at a long time in prison.'

'Oh, thank goodness!'

'And I'm sorry my timing seemed insensitive but you know how it is, Libby. You have to act quickly in these cases.'

'I know, I understand.'

'I'd better go or I'll be late . . .' Stella said, standing up.

'Wait! Stella . . . Do you know . . . ? Do you know what day it is today?'

Stella looked at her, surprised. 'Of course I do, Libby. This would have been the forty-third anniversary of our friendship.'

Libby was dumbfounded – not 'it *is* our forty-third anniversary', but 'it *would have been*'. She watched Stella leave and realised that, unless the journal could clear the whole matter up once and for all, it really was the end of their friendship.

Chapter Twenty-Four

Jersey, December 1941

Queenie's journal

I barely slept, only drifting into a fitful slumber as night turned to day. I was woken by Mama. She was peering at me.

'Oh dear, Queenie, are you not well? It's not like you not to get up. I thought you'd be getting ready for church. Noelle, you're still looking peaky, too. I think the best thing for you both is to stay in bed this morning. Papa and I will go to the service alone. It's parky out there, too, all of a sudden. Bitter wind. No use dragging you two out in this weather. Snuggle down, my loves, and I'll check on you when we get home.'

Mama bustled off in her Sunday best and I turned over, attempting to doze off again, but as soon as the front door slammed shut, Noelle was up and out of bed quick as a flash. I've never seen her like it before – she's usually dreadfully slow to rise. She began pulling on her favourite dress – a nice patterned rayon one – and a lovely wool cardigan the same colour as her eyes. Though we both have brown-red hair, our eyes are very different: mine an unremarkable hazel, while Noelle's are enormous and baby blue.

'What are you up to?' I asked.

'Nothing!' she whispered. 'Go back to sleep!'

But I was too intrigued now. I shifted myself up on the goose-down pillows and observed Noelle pinching her cheeks to redden them and then patting her hair as she gazed at the mirror. She sighed.

'Well, if you're not going to go back to sleep, at least help me get my hair looking decent,' she said, throwing me the hairbrush. I jumped up and Noelle sat on the stool at the dressing table while I practised my new skill – the 'victory roll' hairstyle, named for the air acrobatics the British fighter pilots are said to do when they return victorious from a successful fight with the enemy. I hope Albert isn't getting up to that kind of nonsense, mind you. No point him putting himself in any unnecessary danger! It's a lovely sort of style – half up, with a nice roll keeping the front of the hair off the face and the rest of it falling in waves. I tied the top of an old stocking round Noelle's head like a headband and then rolled the hair over it. By the time I was finished Noelle looked a million dollars and I was wondering what was going on with her.

'You going to tell me, then, now I've done your hair?'

Noelle looked like she was about to let on when there was a banging at the back door. I nearly shrieked with fright. *This is it*, I thought. *They've found the body and they've come to arrest me.* I considered hiding but what use would that be? They'd find me eventually.

'You all right?' asked Noelle. 'You do look pale, like Mama said.'

'I'm fine. I'll just get the door.'

'No need! I'll go . . .' Noelle said, racing down the stairs. I followed her downstairs like a condemned woman but, seeing who was at the door, I felt a huge sense of relief. There, standing in the kitchen in his smart uniform, was Wolfgang. The poor boy looked tired: scarlet fever is continuing to spread amongst the soldiers and he's obviously been working too hard.

'Good morning, Queenie,' Wolfgang said, tearing his eyes away from Noelle and removing his cap. Noelle took it from him and he smiled, immediately looking much brighter. My feelings of relief at the visitor being Wolfgang, rather than soldiers ready to arrest me, were quickly swamped by concern for Noelle. I didn't have time for niceties.

'Noelle, can I speak to you for a moment?' I asked, and she followed me through to the living room. 'What on earth are you doing? You can't have Wolfgang round when Mama and Papa aren't here! It's not respectable!'

'I didn't know he was coming!' Noelle protested, but I gave her a long look.

'Oh, really? You didn't mention that Mama and Papa would be out this morning? And there wasn't any particular reason you got yourself looking all spruce?'

Noelle looked a bit shamefaced. 'Oh, all right, I admit it. I did plan it. But we're not going to be getting up to anything. Wolfgang just wanted to hear me play. He's musical, you see. You can keep us company if you like,' Noelle offered.

'No need for that,' I said grudgingly. 'But I'll be around, so just you remember that! Off you go, then, and apologise to Wolfgang for my rudeness.'

Noelle nodded and was off in a trice, while I went through to the scullery and scrubbed the floor, trying to get rid of my worries through physical exertion. After that, I went back upstairs feeling weary and my worries not remotely allayed. I lay on the bed and started to make a mental list of my suspects.

Mary Jane.

Tommy Le Brun.

Diane.

Rachel Weider.

I suppose that, in their different ways, each of them has a very good reason to have wanted rid of the Grim One but Mary Jane stands out – a

Christmas on the Coast

love affair with him that might have turned sour, judging by the look of her when I bumped into them in the lanes that time. I haven't seen her since then: she's been conspicuous by her absence. I didn't see her at the performance on the final afternoon (clever, if she did kill him) and the Grim One seemed to have had Diane in his sights ever since he came across her at the hair salon. Did Mary Jane know his affections had moved on? They say that hell hath no fury like a woman scorned – and she'd have lost all her Jerrybag perks, to boot. Come to think of it, Mary Jane might have had access to a butcher's knife, too, given the time she spent working at that butcher's in the market a little while ago. But, though she might well have felt upset with the Grim One, would it have been enough to bring her to kill him? Perhaps it was *un crime passionnel* . . .

Then there's Tommy – he's got a temper on him, has Tommy, and he makes no secret of the fact that he loathes the Germans, particularly the bullying ones like the Grim One. He'd have had no shortage of knives either, being the village butcher. My main problem with Tommy as a suspect is that I can't see how he'd have *physically* done it. He was taking part in the show and I was downing brandy with him afterwards. *I'm* his alibi. Unless it all happened when he nipped home to *get* his brandy . . . Could that have been long enough?

Diane is a lovely, sweet lady – looks like she wouldn't harm a fly. But she's clearly not been happy about being on the receiving end of advances from the Grim One and she's already been in a relationship with a thug. Would that make her fuse that much shorter, should she be put in a pressurised situation? She did leave us all early, I remember – before Tommy got back with his brandy. She said she had a headache. Maybe the Grim One followed her and got a bit frisky. There was plenty of heat exchanged between them earlier on. But why on earth would she have had a butcher's knife on her? Where would she have managed to lay her hands on one?

Rachel Weider is a possible candidate, but I confess she feels like a long shot as a suspect. She has every reason in the world to want retribution for the death of her father and her mother's disappearance,

135

but – while the motivation is there for revenge on the Nazis – I can't see why she'd have had the Grim One specifically in her sights. And, having seen how nervous she was in the school attics the other day, I just don't know if she'd have risked being seen out and about. I can't see how *she'd* have got hold of the weapon, either.

Four suspects – but just my own speculations to go on, as things stand. There's only one thing for it: I'm going to have to speak to each of them and conduct my own little secret interviews.

I've just been downstairs to check on Noelle and when I opened the door to the living room slightly, I saw a scene to melt your heart. Noelle was sitting at the piano, straight backed, playing 'Silent Night', while Wolfgang stood beside her, his hand gently resting on her shoulder while he sang with the most soulful voice I've ever heard:

Stille Nacht! Heilige Nacht!
Alles schläft; einsam wacht
Nur das traute hoch heilige Paar.
Holder Knabe im lockigen Haar,
Schlafe in himmlischer Ruh!
Schlafe in himmlischer Ruh!

It was mesmerising. There was something about the scene that made me realise this isn't just a passing fancy between Noelle and Wolfgang – this is the beginning of a love affair. And one, I fear, that can only end in heartbreak.

By the time Mama and Papa returned home, Wolfgang had disappeared again. Noelle and I were sitting at the kitchen table, darning socks and looking like butter wouldn't melt in our mouths.

'Hello, my loves! Oh good, you're both looking much better. You just needed a bit of sleep! Queenie, pet, your father has some exciting news for you!'

I looked up from my sewing, needle and thread poised in the air. Papa smiled.

'We saw Mr and Mrs Ecobichon in church. They've had a message through the Red Cross. From Albert! They want to show it to you, so they've invited you for tea today. We said yes on your behalf. You need to be there for three o'clock.'

'What did it say? The message?' I asked.

'No idea, but they'll tell you soon enough,' said Mama. 'Now another bit of good news is that Papa's friend, old Helier, has given us a bit of wrasse for our lunch. He's got some understanding with a couple of German soldiers, who let him fish down on the rocks as long as he gives half his catch to them. He's a crafty devil, that one! Brave, as well. He was one of the fishermen who helped evacuate troops from St Malo shortly after Dunkirk. More than twenty thousand men saved! He's a decent fellow. And God bless him, he's given us some seawater we can boil for salt to preserve our Christmas pork as well. I'd better get preparing the fish now. I'm sure it's good news, Queenie – the Ecobichons looked very happy.'

At three o'clock on the dot, I arrived at the farmhouse just up the road from us. Mrs Ecobichon greeted me at the door and smiled, her eyes crinkling behind tortoiseshell spectacles. It was nice to see her so cheery, as it doesn't often happen: Albert's parents aren't really like my own, who are ever so warm and hospitable. Though Mr Ecobichon does take a drink with Papa in the pub every so often, and they sometimes dine with us at the farmhouse, the Ecobichons tend to keep themselves to themselves a bit more; they're a little bit stiff and polite. But I was touched by the warmth of their welcome on this occasion, which included a kitchen table laid with a generous spread, including bread, jam and even a homemade cake!

'Come and sit down,' Mrs Ecobichon said, after she'd taken my coat. I took a seat and patted my hair – I'd put it up in a 'victory roll' after my success with Noelle's in the morning. It was dreadfully quiet in the kitchen – Mrs Ecobichon has never been very good at making conversation – and the tick of the kitchen clock and the clatter of mint-green china seemed to highlight our silence. Fortunately, a moment later the door through to the living room burst open and Albert's little sisters all came bounding in at once. Kitty, who's fourteen and has just discovered romantic fiction, was upon me in an instant.

'Oh, Queenie, I'm so pleased to see you! I so loved *Wuthering Heights*. I have it here for you. Do you have another I could borrow? Please say you do!'

'Of course,' I promised. 'I'll have a look when I get home and drop something off for you tomorrow.'

'Something suitable though, Queenie, you will make sure of that?' said Mrs Ecobichon, as she poured carrot tea for us all.

'I promise,' I told her, then I winked at Kitty. By then I'd been besieged by the twins – they're only six and a real handful. Connie and Daisy, they're called, and I can't for the life of me tell which one is which. They don't seem to mind, though.

'Piggyback! Piggyback!' they demanded in unison and, obliging as ever, I heaved one of them onto my back and chugged around the room with her, then – once she was safely deposited on a kitchen chair – picked up the other little girl and trotted around once more.

'Again!' Connie or Daisy demanded when they'd both had a turn.

'Poor Queenie needs a sit down now,' Mrs Ecobichon told them. 'Now go and get your pa and tell him our guest is here.'

Shortly, Mr Ecobichon joined us and we all tucked into the tea, the girls much quieter in their father's company. He's a good man, Mr Ecobichon, but he can be quite stern. I kept wondering when they were going to tell me about Albert. Finally, once I'd finished my tea, Mrs Ecobichon rose from her chair, went to the dresser and brought me an envelope. I studied it, enjoying the anticipation, and, with all eyes on me, I lifted out the piece of paper within. It was more like a form than a letter, with Albert's name at the top under the heading 'Sender', then the message, beneath which was the date (six months the message had taken to arrive!) and details of the addressee, with space for a reply on the back. There was a blue streak across the form. It's true, then, what they say: the Germans do check for invisible ink. I returned to the heading 'Message' and read:

Hope you and girls are well. I'm exhausted, but fine. Send Queenie fondest love. I pray for her and you all every day. Yours, Albert.

I felt tears well up in my eyes: a mixture of relief – he was alive and well and thinking of me – and despair, since it was such a short note, with no details at all. Of course, the missives are limited to only twenty-five words and heavily censored should anyone try to offer more than the bare necessities, but still . . . I wanted to know how he'd survived the Battle of Britain and the blitz; how he lived day to day; what he ate; where he slept; how he *felt*. But for now, I would have to be satisfied with these brief tidings. It was certainly better than nothing.

I left very soon after that, keen to get home before it was completely dark. As I pulled on my coat, Mrs Ecobichon pressed a brief kiss onto my forehead. She'd never done that before. I cycled home, filled with love and a renewed sense of well-being, but as I headed down the hill, passing by the little path where I'd found the Grim One, I saw there was a right commotion going on, with soldiers all shouting to one another in German. *Oh, good heavens*, I thought to myself, with dread again replacing my short-lived burst of happiness. *They must have just found the body!*

I sped past, quick as I could, arriving home out of breath and hastily locking the farmhouse door behind me.

This is it. The reprisals will now begin.

Chapter Twenty-Five

Jersey, December 2016

Liberty

The day didn't improve. The afternoon involved meeting a highly unreasonable deadline and by the time Libby left the office it was nearly seven. She got home to find the house a mess, with no sign of any supper being prepared.

'At last! There you are!' beamed Liam, muting whatever he was watching on the TV. He was surrounded by crisp packets and cans of drink. 'What's for dinner? I'm starving!'

'I've no idea. Where's Dad?' Libby asked, dumping her bag and flicking through the post on the hall table – three brown envelopes and nothing remotely interesting-looking. Not even any Christmas cards.

'He and Milo went to pick up the tree from Didier.' That was something, at least, thought Libby. Ignoring Liam's request to bring through some snacks, she trudged up the stairs and turned right towards the bathroom. A nice bath was exactly what she needed before she set about making supper. She ran the taps, pouring in her favourite bath salts, then undressed and plunged herself into the tub.

'Arrrgh!' she yelled, jumping straight back out again. The bathwater was freezing cold. 'Liam, why is there no hot water?' she shouted downstairs.

'Oh, sorry, Mum! I had a bath earlier and Milo had a shower. I forgot to put the immersion on.'

Libby stomped towards the airing cupboard and flicked the immersion heater on, before retreating to the bedroom to dress in leggings and her favourite sloppy jumper. She was just about to head downstairs when she saw Amy's carrier bags in the corner of the room. She sighed, retrieving the Christmas wrapping paper from behind her dressing table. She'd already asked Amy to resend the text so she was able to wrap each of the gifts (which she had to admit were lovely and actually very thoughtful) and then label it appropriately.

Back down in the kitchen, she searched in the fridge and, finding only eggs and mushrooms, decided on omelette. She was in the process of chopping the mushrooms when the back door burst open and a gaggle of family members appeared: Milo first, looking gloomy despite his festive outing, then Henry carrying an enormous tree and – bringing up the rear – Amy.

'Amy! What are you doing here? I thought you were working on some huge case and we wouldn't see you till Christmas Eve?'

'Where shall I put this?' interrupted Henry.

'Sitting room, of course, where we always put it,' Libby replied tersely. She looked at Amy enquiringly.

'Oh, the case settled!' Amy said, smiling. 'Huge relief! I can relax now.'

'But I wrapped your presents! You said you'd be too busy!'

'Well, I thought I would be. Thanks so much. I hate wrapping! I always think it'll be really fun and Christmassy and then it's just uncomfortable and boring!'

'It certainly is,' Libby agreed, using her knife with some force on the unsuspecting mushrooms.

'Oh no, are you making omelette?' asked Amy. 'But you know I don't like eggs!'

'Amy, I didn't know you were coming for supper. You said you'd see me on Christmas Eve! And there isn't anything else, so it's this or nothing.'

Amy sighed. 'I'll just make myself some toast, then,' she muttered. 'Oh, bloody hell! The bread's mouldy!'

Libby ignored her. 'Liam!' she shouted through to the sitting room. 'Can you come and lay the table and open some wine?'

'I'm just helping Dad with the tree!'

Libby threw down the knife and set about laying the table herself, then opened the wine while the butter started to sizzle in the pan. Finally, all was ready.

'Supper's up!' she said, and, as usual, everyone took so long to come to the table that the meal was tepid by the time they began to eat.

'Delicious!' said Henry, washing his cold omelette down with some wine.

'Mum, you know I asked for a new iPad for Christmas? Can I get a PlayStation 4 instead?' Milo asked, suddenly piping up.

'Milo,' said Libby, speaking as calmly as she could. 'You do realise it's the twenty-second of December? It's too late to go changing your mind about Christmas presents.'

'What? But that's so unfair!'

'Unfair? Do any of you really appreciate what's fair and unfair in this life? You know, I'm reading my great-aunt's journal at the moment, from Christmas 1941 when the island was occupied by the Germans, and you wouldn't believe what life was like in Jersey then. Barely anything to eat, nothing in the shops, very little entertainment and living in constant fear for your life. You kids don't know you're born!'

Libby watched Liam roll his eyes and felt herself losing it. She was like a volcano erupting. 'Don't you *dare* roll your eyes at me! You know what you are? You're spoilt! All three of you are. And the worst thing of all is that I know it's all my fault. If I could send you back to Christmas 1941 for a day, right now, then I jolly well would!'

'Libby, calm down, dear!' said Henry, looking worried.

'And don't you "dear" me, either!' she yelled, turning on him. 'In fact, it's not just my fault they're like this. It's your fault, too! All of you constantly just taking, taking, taking. Well, I've had enough. I've got nothing left to give. If you want Christmas this year, then you lot organise it, because I quit!'

And with that, Libby made her exit, thundering up the stairs as four gobsmacked faces gawped at each other in disbelief.

Chapter Twenty-Six

QUEENIE'S JOURNAL

Thankfully there was no knock at the door for me last night, but gossip has been tearing around the parish like wildfire. This morning, Papa came in and relayed the news he'd just heard up in the village. I was busy ironing when he burst in the back door.

'A body's been found in the parish!' he told me. 'The Germans found it yesterday and apparently it belongs to that nasty officer fellow who worked for the *Feldkommandantur* – the one we all called the Grim One. I bumped into Phyllis Bisson and she said they've started a murder investigation! The man was stabbed!'

I was trembling at his words. I had to put the iron down. 'Do they have a suspect?' I asked.

'Apparently so,' Papa replied, and I felt a little relieved at the thought I might be off the hook. But I was horrified by what Papa told me next. 'They're blaming the escaped Russian. They think it was Oleg,' he whispered, even though we were in the privacy of our own home. 'The walls have ears,' Papa's always saying nowadays. He lit his pipe with an unsteady hand.

'Oleg?' I whispered back. 'But he wouldn't hurt a fly! I mean, I know the Grim One treated him badly but he . . . he just wouldn't have. I know it.'

'Course he didn't do it,' Papa agreed, speaking in low tones now, rather than a whisper. 'I know for certain he didn't do it. According to Mrs Bisson, the Germans say the Grim One was killed on Saturday afternoon – around the time of the pantomime. And Oleg was with Mrs Lucas the whole afternoon. Mama and I had arranged to go round there straight from watching you perform, to report on the final show, and Mrs Lucas told us she and Oleg had been playing chess to while away the time until we arrived. But of course nobody can vouch for Oleg because nobody's meant to know where he is. The worry is that the Germans are going to step up their search for him now, which puts all of us in danger. There's even talk of them using bloodhounds to hunt him down! They'll be on a rampage before we know it. I'm going to head round to Mrs Lucas immediately. She needs to make sure Oleg's well hidden at all times from now on.'

Mama came into the kitchen at this point with a basketful of damp washing. She'd attempted to put it all out on the line but the prevailing westerly wind had driven in enormous great rain clouds and it had just started to bucket down. It was only mid-morning but almost as dark as night. 'Will you tell Mama the news?' Papa asked me, and I nodded, while he dashed off next door to warn Mrs Lucas.

'Well, blow me down with a feather!' Mama remarked, collapsing onto a chair at the shock of the news. 'A murder! In Jersey! And a German officer . . . This doesn't bode well for any of us, least of all that poor Russian if he's found. There'll be all sorts of repercussions from this, you mark my words,' Mama said, nodding sagely at her own foretelling.

She wasn't wrong. By this afternoon, we'd received news in the *Evening Post* that until the murderer is found the curfew will be from seven in the evening until seven the next morning! Twelve whole hours! Not only that, but the extra Christmas rations we've been anticipating have now been shelved. That's a real blow for everyone. It'll put a real dampener on Christmas. I immediately thought of Kitty and the twins, who would've so loved having a little bit of chocolate on Christmas Day.

There was a warning in the paper, too – anyone who's found to have helped the escaped Russian in any way will be held to account. They're even offering a reward for anyone who comes forward with information as to his whereabouts and that's put the wind up us as a family. We sat around the dinner table tonight, trying to work out exactly who knows that Mrs Lucas is hiding Oleg. The four of us, of course, and Mr and Mrs Ecobichon . . . Then Noelle made a confession.

'I'm really sorry,' she said, as we all toyed with our turnip soup. 'But I told someone . . . about Oleg.' My heart immediately sank as I imagined her confiding in Wolfgang.

'Who did you tell?' Papa asked sternly.

'Sybil,' Noelle admitted. 'We were chatting the other day and I don't know how, but it just slipped out and then I felt terrible! I swore her to secrecy!'

Papa smiled. 'Good grief! You don't need to worry about Sybil,' he assured Noelle. 'Her family is hiding the Jewish girl! They're not going to be blabbing to anyone about Oleg when they've got Rachel Weider up in their attics! But Noelle, please, you mustn't just let it slip to anyone else, all right? Especially your German friend. This is serious now. We're all implicated. If we're found to have helped harbour a Russian slave worker – let alone one who's suspected of murdering a German officer – we'll be packed off to a concentration camp without time to say goodbye to Lenny the cat. Do you understand?'

'Yes, Papa,' Noelle replied, her eyes full of tears. She was trembling and I squeezed her hand and offered her what I hoped was a reassuring smile, though my own legs had turned to jelly under the table. Knowing that Oleg is a suspect has made me even more adamant about finding out who the real murderer is. I'm beginning my investigation tomorrow, starting with Tommy.

Chapter Twenty-Seven

Jersey, December 2016

Liberty

Libby woke up with a feeling resembling a hangover. She felt guilty after the previous evening's outburst but she was still angry. She decided to creep off to work without facing any of the family. She threw herself into her job all day long but at five o'clock she knew it was time to leave and return home to face the music.

She pulled on her coat and was just turning off her computer when Farty appeared at her desk. 'Leaving already?' he asked, checking his watch.

'I've stayed late the last couple of days. There's no conference call set up with the American team today, is there?'

'Well, no, but you're not back now until the New Year, and there are a few more things I need doing before you go . . .'

'Are they vital? Like, life or death?' Libby asked him, and Farty looked shocked.

'No, I suppose not . . .'

'Then I'm afraid they'll have to wait. Merry Christmas!' she replied, and, as she strode off towards the lift, Libby decided she was rather enjoying being as straight-talking as Stella. She'd been a people-pleaser for far too long.

She crossed the road, thinking to take a shortcut past the Court, through the Royal Square, but she couldn't help but stop when she saw the festive scene in front of her. The fairy lights in all the trees were twinkling, the branches swishing about in the strong wind, and in the middle of the square a talented choir, surrounded by warmly wrapped-up islanders, was belting out Christmas carols. Suddenly feeling in no rush to get home, Libby joined the crowd. Some kindly old lady wearing a bobble hat passed her a sheet. 'Hark the herald angels sing, "Glory to the newborn King!"' Libby sang, unable to stop herself smiling.

Then a beautiful young soloist began to sing 'Ave Maria' and Libby found herself mesmerised by the innocent voice. As she looked around at all the jolly people, clasping mulled wine and enjoying the laid-back concert, she thought of Queenie's journal and how, after the murder, the authorities had withdrawn the promise of extra Christmas rations and increased the nightly curfew as punishment. Yet, despite their best efforts, the Nazi regime hadn't managed to quash the island's spirit and her ancestors had carried on as best they could. She wondered how many of the people standing in the square now, swaying to the emotive music, were the same brave islanders who'd somehow managed to live through five years of occupation, or at least descendants of them.

The girl's solo came to an end, to uproarious applause. 'Would you like some mulled wine?' the lady in the bobble hat asked. 'We've got a sing-along to festive favourites in a minute. You know, "Frosty the Snowman" and so on.'

'No thanks, that's kind of you,' Libby replied. 'But I must get on. Lots to do!'

'Well, thank you for stopping by. Have a lovely Christmas!'

'And you!'

Libby hurried through the square and onto Mulcaster Street, heading past the Royal Yacht Hotel on her way to the car park. But again she found herself waylaid as she spotted the markets at the Weighbridge – all part of La Fête dé Noué, Jersey's annual Christmas festival. It was impossible not to be drawn in by it all and she knew then that, despite her heated remarks the previous evening, there was no way she was really going to cancel Christmas.

She meandered from stall to stall, buying some lovely handcrafted earrings as stocking fillers for Amy and some irresistible-looking cheese from one of the French stalls. She checked her watch – six o'clock. She really did need to head home. Making her way past the Pomme d'Or – the hotel that had been requisitioned as German naval headquarters during the occupation – she found that she was no longer dreading her return home to face the aftermath of her outburst the night before. She loved Jersey. And she loved her family. She just wanted to get home and make things right in time for Christmas.

Chapter Twenty-Eight

Jersey, December 1941

Queenie's journal

It's the 23rd of December and today I managed to interview both Tommy and Diane. Without them knowing, of course! I was just finishing with the posh lady from one of the manors when Tommy came stomping into the salon like a bull in a china shop, his face puce with rage.

'Morning, Tommy!' I called to him. 'Can I help?'

'I doubt it!' he replied. 'Got any influence with the Germans? Able to get them to change that blasted curfew?'

I hadn't a clue what he was on about but I showed my customer to the till, dealt with payment (Reichsmarks nowadays) and then turned to Tommy. He'd clearly come into the salon to let off a bit of steam but both Odette and Sabine were busy, which left me to deal with him. He was wringing his hands in anger.

'What's the matter?' I asked.

'It's my girl. You know my lass Stéphanie had her little nipper a month early, eh? Didn't think she could have babies but the doctor says all that weight she's lost since the Jerries got here helped. Only good thing to come of the blasted Nazis! Didn't stop the baby coming early, mind, and now the Jerries have changed the curfew, she can't get into the hospital to feed the little wretch. The doctor says the boy's doing well; he should be all right. But I'm not so sure. A baby, especially an early one like that – he needs his mother's milk . . .'

'I'm sure he'll be fine,' I tried to reassure him. 'Look, come and have a cup of coffee. Not the real thing, but Sabine's been busy roasting parsnips and it's not too bad.'

Tommy followed me through to the back and plonked himself down on a chair while I made the drinks.

'What do you make of all that business with the murder, then?' I asked.

'That rotten Nazi deserved everything he got! *Mouôn Doue d'la vie*, you know what he did the very day he died, eh? He went to that florist's in St Peter and told Mrs Bouchard he wanted some purple orchids. Rare as hen's teeth at this time of year, eh, especially nowadays, but a special request from the grieving family of Cyril De St Croix meant Mrs Bouchard had managed to get hold of them for Cyril's funeral. When Mrs Bouchard refused to sell them to the Grim One, the pig got on the phone to the *Kommandant*, then told Mrs Bouchard she had a choice: either she could sell him the flowers or he'd shut down her shop for a week! Well, times are hard . . . She had no choice . . . Guess who he gave the flowers to, eh? Not Mary Jane, I'll tell you that much.'

'Diane?'

Tommy looked a bit cheated that I'd managed to guess first time. 'She didn't even want the damn things. It was the day of the final show. Same day the Grim One was killed. She took the flowers back to the florist's, eh, and fortunately it wasn't too late for the funeral.'

'That was good of her. So who do you think did it, then?' I have to admit to myself that I don't have quite the subtlety I'd anticipated when it comes to conducting my criminal investigations.

'Well, it wasn't me – that much I can tell you! If it was, I'd be proud to let you know, eh. No . . . my money's on Diane. You know she once tried to stab that good-for-nothing husband of hers? Though that's not how he died. At least, I don't think it was . . . My word, you don't think she's a mass murderer, do you?'

'I very much doubt it,' I replied, trying to suppress a smile. 'But how on earth would she have got hold of a butcher's knife? That was the weapon, wasn't it?'

'So they say. These days, if you've got the right contacts, you can lay your hands on a fair bit of illicit gear on the black market, eh. If Diane needed a butcher's knife, she could have got it on the sly, no questions asked. I sold a couple to that Bob character from town myself to try to raise a bit of cash.'

I hadn't thought of that and it didn't help rule out any of my suspects. But, from talking to Tommy, I was fairly sure it wasn't him. Not least because, in many ways, as he said to me, killing the Grim One would have been a badge of honour for him.

It was under rather less usual circumstances that I managed to interview Diane herself in the afternoon. I bumped into her down at St Brelade's Bay, where I was searching for holly to decorate the house. It grows well in the churchyard in St Brelade and it's our tradition to go there just before Christmas to pick some. It must be the graveyard with the best view in Jersey: a bit wasted on the residents! A lovely sweep of golden bay, the sea turquoise in summer, reaching all the way from the church across to Ouaisné.

I usually have Noelle for company but she's still not fully recovered, so I took the bus down to the bay on my own. I wasn't alone for long, though. Reaching up for a branch of lush green leaves and red berries, I heard a voice behind me.

'Hello, Queenie, what you up to?'

I turned around and couldn't believe my luck when I saw it was Diane. She had a bundle of garments in her arms.

'Just picking some holly to make the farmhouse a bit more festive,' I replied.

'I'll come and 'elp you. I'm just dropping off some surplices I mended for the vicar. Give me two minutes and I'll be with you.'

True to her word, she was back moments later.

''Ere, I'm taller than you. Let me get those bits for you.'

'Thanks,' I grinned, passing her the secateurs.

'Ain't 'alf brisk today,' she commented as she snipped away, while I popped the holly into my basket. 'That wind's ever so bitter.'

'They say it's going to drop again before Christmas. At least it's been mild until now,' I replied. 'There's even some daffodils out on the farm. I've never known that happen before at Christmas.'

All of a sudden, the staccato rattle of gunfire and the drone of a plane drowned out our chat. The noise grew louder and we looked up to see what was happening.

'Oh my goodness!' I shouted. 'It's a British fighter plane! The Germans are shooting at it! Quick, let's head down to the beach!'

We abandoned everything and ran along the path through the graveyard, then down the slipway onto the beach. Fortunately, it's well known that the bay isn't a mined area, so we were able to make our way to the shoreline. By now, the plane was spiralling down towards the water, billowing smoke and making all sorts of terrible noises.

'Oh, that poor pilot!' Diane said, squinting up towards the sky. ''E'll never survive this.' But a moment later, we saw a parachute open up and a man drift gently down towards the water.

'Well, he might escape being set on fire in the plane but he'll drown unless someone helps him!' I said. We looked around and could see a number of people heading down towards the beach, but we were the closest by far.

Rebecca Boxall

''Ere, 'old these,' said Diane, as she quickly shrugged off her coat and shoes. Then, hesitating for only a moment, she took off her skirt and blouse, too. She ran into the water in just her slip and brassiere and, after wading through the shallows, swam with astonishing efficiency in the direction of the pilot. He was a couple of hundred yards away and looked to be in distress, all tangled up in his parachute. Five minutes later, Diane was pulling the man out of the water. He was coughing and spluttering, trying to disentangle himself, but he was alive. A crowd had gathered down by the water by now, surrounding the three of us.

'There's a couple of Jerries heading down from the hotel over there. You know – where they have that German NAAFI,' a young boy warned, his voice breathless with fear and excitement as he made reference to the army's recreational area. 'Are you going to run?' he asked the pilot.

'No,' the man said, out of breath. 'I won't run, but you better had,' he said, looking at Diane with some urgency. Though he wasn't looking his best, drenched and shocked, he was handsome all right. I saw him and Diane take each other in and there was an instant spark between them. I wasn't surprised: could there have been a more romantic meeting than that?

'Please!' the man begged. 'You've saved my life. Now save your own. Please run! I'll never forget what you just did for me. My name is Glen. Glen Bailey. And yours?' he asked hurriedly.

'I'm Diane,' she said as she pulled her clothes back on, her cheeks reddening as she realised she had quite an audience considering her state of undress. 'I'm widowed,' she added. I smiled at this.

'Come on!' I said, spotting the German soldiers racing towards the crowd and I grabbed Diane's hand. We ran but the soldiers didn't follow us. Their priority was the pilot.

By the time we reached the churchyard, Diane was shivering.

'How did you get here?' I asked.

'The bus.'

'Me, too. If we're quick, we'll be in time for the ten past three. You need to get yourself home and nice and dry before you catch a chill.'

'Let's go, then,' Diane said, grabbing my arm as we raced off towards the bus stop. Though clearly very cold, she was smiling. Then she frowned. 'What'll 'appen to 'im?' she asked. ''E'll be all right, won't 'e?'

'He won't be very comfortable but he should survive,' I tried to assure her. 'He'll be a prisoner of war now, but at least he's alive – thanks to you.'

When we reached the stop in St Ouen's village, I hopped off with Diane and walked with her along to her house. It was only then that I realised I hadn't actually asked her any questions about the murder. She needed to get inside and warm up, so I kept it brief.

'Diane?' I asked, as she reached towards her front door. 'Can I ask? I'm sorry to intrude on your private life but that officer – the Grim One. What went on between you? I saw a commotion between you just before the last performance at the panto . . . I hoped you were all right . . .'

Diane looked left and right, then beckoned me inside. 'Come and 'ave a cuppa,' she said. 'Not a decent one, of course, but I've got some bramble-leaf.'

I followed her in. The house was deathly silent and I felt for her then as I thought how loud and busy it must have been all the while her children had been living there. Diane nipped off to change, then she brought in some water for the kettle and busied herself making the tea while I sat at the kitchen table. A framed photograph of her two children was propped up on the dresser, next to a display of pretty china. They sat in an upright, formal stance, one behind the other, but both were smiling broadly. It was enough to break your heart, seeing that picture there in that immaculate house. It was far too neat and tidy for a family home. Diane poured the tea from a pot dressed in a lovely knitted tea cosy, then sat down opposite me at the table.

Rebecca Boxall

''E was *interested* in me,' she said, with a pained look on her face. 'And I weren't interested back. I know a bully when I see one, after all I went through with me 'usband . . . I 'ave to admit, when I 'eard the Grim One 'ad been killed, I felt a sodding great sense of relief. 'E were persistent, that man. 'E tried it on with me – the final afternoon of the show. I had to slap 'im, to get 'im off me. That's why I was in tears when you came to get your make-up done. I was terrified the rest of the evening. Kept thinkin' I'd end up arrested by the end of the night . . . 'Alfway through the show, 'e found me in the wings and 'e was full of threats, tellin' me it was an offence not only to 'ave assaulted 'im by giving 'im a slap but also to 'ave "insulted German forces". In other words, I'd committed a crime by rejecting 'is advances!'

'Is that why you went home?'

'Yes. Said I 'ad an 'eadache and no word of a lie, that was. A real belter. But I wanted to get back to the safety of me own 'ome, too, quick as I could. I was worried. Either 'e was goin' to try it on again or 'e'd get me arrested. I've never been so relieved to reach my 'ouse as I was that night.'

'So you didn't come across him then, on your way home?'

'No, thank the Lord. Queenie, you don't think it was me, do you? That I killed 'im?'

'Of course not!' I told her, but still, after I'd thanked her for the tea and started to head home, a grain of doubt lingered in my mind. After all, she'd had even more reason than I'd first thought to end the Grim One's life. If he hadn't died that evening, he'd almost certainly have carried on pestering her – or had her arrested. And if she'd ended up imprisoned in Europe, she might well have never seen her children again.

156

Chapter Twenty-Nine

Jersey, December 2016

Liberty

As Libby pulled up at the Vicarage, she saw that the drive was full of cars: Henry's was there and Amy's sporty little convertible was parked up next to Liam's rusty old Toyota Corolla. As she approached the house, she realised she felt a little nervous.

Bracing herself, she opened the front door.

'Hello!' she called out. Nothing. No sounds at all, though the house felt lovely and warm. There were nice smells, too. Someone had been baking. She left her handbag in the hall and opened the door to the sitting room.

'Surprise!' they all shouted. Libby laughed as all four of them launched themselves across the room to hug her. Libby stood back and looked around her.

'I can't believe it!' she said. 'It's all so beautiful. The fire and the tree and the decorations! Presents under the tree, all these lovely candles! And it's so tidy!'

'We're so sorry,' Liam said, 'for being such spoilt brats. It was harsh, the talking-to you gave us, but completely justified. We decided to pull together and get everything organised. The food shop's done and we've all been cooking and baking.'

'Oh, Liam, was it your idea? You lovely boy!'

'Actually, it wasn't. It was Milo's.'

Libby looked at her younger son, who was standing by the fire looking embarrassed. He shrugged and Libby felt her heart might burst with love.

'It's true, Milo was the one to suggest it,' Amy chipped in. 'None of us wanted to admit it to start with, but the truth is we *have* been taking you for granted – me especially. I've been such a cow, getting stressed about trying to juggle the wedding and my job and taking it out on you. I'm just so sorry, Mum.'

'It doesn't matter,' Libby smiled. 'It doesn't matter at all. We're here, all together and all pulling together. Just in time for Christmas.'

'Will Stella be joining us on Christmas Day, Mum, like she always does?' asked Liam.

'I'm not sure,' Libby replied, a dark cloud threatening to eclipse this sunny moment. She decided not to think about it. 'Listen, it's not that I don't trust you, but would it be okay if I just had a little look at what you bought?' After all, the list in Libby's handbag was as long as her arm and she couldn't help but doubt that her family – unused to grocery shopping – would have managed to remember everything they'd need for the days ahead.

Everyone laughed and followed Libby through to the kitchen, then stood silently, looking nervous, while Libby inspected the contents of first the larder and then the fridge. Libby ticked items off in her head as she registered them. Cranberry sauce, bread sauce, stuffing, bacon, brown bread to go with the salmon she'd bought. Lemons? Amazingly, yes. Potatoes, carrots, peas, sprouts, mince pies (homemade!), trifle (ditto!), oranges, brandy, wine . . . The cupboards were groaning.

She closed her eyes and thought for a moment. It wasn't that she was *trying* to catch them out, but there were an awful lot of things to think of at Christmastime. 'Crackers?' she asked. Amy dashed through to the sitting room and returned waving a box triumphantly. Libby smiled. 'Champagne?' was her final question.

'Abso-bloody-lutely!' Liam laughed, and he ran through to the garage, returning with a very decent bottle and starting to uncork it.

'Hang on, let me get the flutes,' said Henry, in a fluster as he grabbed them out of the corner cupboard. 'Steady as she goes . . .' he said as he carefully poured the frothing liquid into the glasses. Then – having each claimed a drink (a thimbleful for Milo, too) – they trooped back through to the sitting room and waited patiently for Libby's verdict.

'I can't fault you!' she said, taking a sip of bubbles. 'I'm completely blown away,' she added, a lump in her throat. 'You really have done me proud.'

And she watched as each of her family exchanged little looks that spoke of all their hard work having well and truly paid off.

Chapter Thirty

Christmas Eve and, as predicted, the wind has dropped, leaving this corner of the island still and silent. I woke early and left Noelle slumbering in bed, pausing as always on the landing to check the state of the sea from the window. Low tide, which – though generous with its landscape of sharp black rocks – brings an insidious stench of seaweed into the house.

Papa was already out in the fields but Mama was in the kitchen. She had the wireless on and was whistling along to various carols while she attempted to make pastry with our meagre rations.

'What I wouldn't do for a great tub of butter,' she remarked, smiling, when I appeared in the doorway. 'Though at least we're able to make our own from the milk. You're up early!' she added, seeing I was dressed and ready for the day.

'You know how I've always loved Christmas Eve. Didn't want to waste it. Though it feels different now, doesn't it? I don't think I ever properly appreciated those Christmases before the war. Even if the island wasn't occupied, it'd be hard to get into the spirit properly knowing Albert's out there fighting for us.'

'Oh, Queenie, my love, you sound down in the dumps. It's not the same, you're right, but we'll make the best of it and, by next year, with any luck we'll be back to normal again. Those Jerries will have been chased out and Albert will be back with us. Come here, now, and give me a hug.'

I managed a smile and one of Mama's great big cuddles had the right effect on me. 'Do you need a hand with the baking?' I asked.

'No, my love, I've got it all under control. It's not exactly going to be a feast but we'll be eating better than a lot of the poor souls on the island. Actually, I've got another basket of food for Sybil's family. I don't suppose you'd have time to drop it off before you head to the salon, would you?'

'Of course!' I said, pleased that I'd been given a valid reason to see Rachel. I wolfed down a bit of breakfast, then grabbed my coat and the basket and cycled along Route des Havres before puffing up the hill towards Violet's school. It was quiet as anything up there, being the Christmas holidays, and it took a little while for Sybil to come to the door of the school.

'Queenie, thank goodness it's just you. I was making sure Rachel had time to hide. Let's go up quickly. You're so kind to have brought us more food . . . How's Noelle?'

'She's much better, thanks, but sleeping a lot still.'

'Tell her I'll pop down this afternoon. About time we had another gossip – last time I saw her she was full of news. Told me about the Russian you're helping to hide and her German doctor! She sounds like she's ever so sweet on him! I'll bring some music with me and we can play a duet. Will you tell her?'

When we reached the attics, Sybil disappeared off and I knocked gently on the door to the room where I knew Rachel was hiding. 'Rachel, it's me – Queenie.'

Rachel seemed even worse than last time – so gaunt and pale and solemn. She had large circles under her eyes and, unsurprisingly, there was a hunted look about her.

'Queenie! It's so wonderful to see you,' she said, hugging me. She felt as fragile as a little bird. 'Come in, come and have a chat . . .'

'You look tired,' I said, and then wished I hadn't. I hate it when people say that to me: makes me feel a hundred times worse.

'I'm not sleeping much since I heard about that murder. I'm worried the Germans are going to go on a rampage to find whoever did it.'

'Do you know who the main suspect is?' I asked.

'The Russian slave worker, isn't it? Sybil told me you're helping to hide him.'

'That's right . . . It wasn't him, though. Papa knows Oleg couldn't have done it. Makes you wonder who it might have been.'

'Sybil and I have been saying the same. She was up in the attics with me the afternoon it happened. It was so kind of her. I know she wanted to go and see the final performance of your pantomime – her parents went – but she didn't want me to be alone, so she stayed here with me and we played cards.'

I'd never really thought Rachel would have been the murderer – she's too gentle and has too much to lose – though I'd wanted to eliminate her from my suspicions. And she'd told me what I needed to hear – she had an alibi.

'Have you been out at all since you came here?' I asked, just to be sure.

'Not once!' she told me. 'I haven't even left the attics. I just can't risk it. If I want to survive, I have to stay here and just hope to goodness the war finishes soon . . .'

I hugged her hard. 'This stupid war,' I whispered, a lump in my throat. 'You'll be free soon . . . I'm sure of it,' I said, though in truth I wasn't so certain.

I had to get to work then – plenty of customers wanting to look spruce for Christmas – but it was early closing, so I arrived home by three. Papa finished up in the yard and decided to light the fire early, so we all settled down in the living room to listen to Noelle play for us.

'Sybil said she'd come and join you,' I said, remembering. 'You can play some duets.'

'What time?' asked Noelle, scrabbling about and finding some music from inside the piano stool.

'This afternoon, she said. She'll be here soon, I'd have thought.' We heard a knock at the door. 'Maybe that's her now,' I said, though the next moment my heart leapt as I heard raised male voices shouting '*Öffne die Tür!*' and then, without waiting for us to open the door, the sound of heavy-booted footsteps charging into the kitchen.

'Queenie, quick – through that door and hide till you hear them head upstairs. Then go and warn Mrs Lucas!' Papa whispered. I darted through the little door next to the fireplace and stood with my back against the wall in the hallway while I waited. I heard the soldiers upturning the kitchen table and chairs and then rushing through to the living room. Thankfully, it didn't sound like they had any dogs with them.

'Stay here, all of you!' they barked to Mama, Papa and Noelle. I could hear furniture being thrown about in there and the bureau drawers being opened and closed. One of the soldiers shouted some orders and I could hear the men thunder up the stairs. This was my cue. I ran through to the kitchen, horrified at the mess (Mama's pies were scattered on the floor!), then pulled open the back door.

I came face to face with Wolfgang.

'What is going on?' he asked, seeing the state of the kitchen.

'There are soldiers here,' I whispered. 'They're searching the house. They're looking for an escaped Russian, I think.'

'And where are you going?' he asked, eyebrows raised.

'I just need to . . . to do something,' I said, hopelessly vague. Time was running out and Wolfgang was blocking my exit. I looked at him desperately. 'Please . . .' I breathed. 'Wolfgang, please . . .' He nodded, almost imperceptibly, then stood to one side. I ran, fast as I could, arriving breathless at Mrs Lucas's house. I hammered on the back door and Mrs Lucas opened the door, looking scared to death.

'Queenie!' she said, registering my alarm. 'What is it?'

'They're searching our house. They'll be here next. Papa said to warn you!'

'Thank you,' she answered. She turned immediately and took the stairs briskly to the first floor. I followed her. 'Where is he?' I asked. 'Where's he hiding?'

'He's studying. In the guest bedroom.'

We burst into the room. Oleg took one look at us and paled.

'You know what to do, Oleg,' said Mrs Lucas. Amazingly efficient under this extreme threat, she took him through to her bedroom, then pulled up the carpet next to her bed and rattled some floorboards with her foot. 'These ones,' she said, and I helped her lift them while Oleg lay down and contorted himself into the space underneath. We covered his terrified face with the boards and pulled the carpet back. I only hoped he'd be able to breathe. Then we dashed back to the other room and found his writing paper and pencils. Mrs Lucas grabbed everything and hastened downstairs to the living room, where the fire was already lit. She threw the evidence onto it and we watched as the papers burned. My heart was galloping.

'Now you must go,' said Mrs Lucas. 'Head home and try to look like you're just arriving back from the salon,' she advised. I nodded and left through the front just as I heard the back door burst open.

Everyone was in the kitchen when I arrived home and, for the first time in my life, I saw Mama in tears. 'Don't worry, Mama,' I said, rubbing her back while she sobbed. Papa had Noelle in his arms. 'He's well hidden, I promise. I'm sure they won't find him. And we can clear this mess up in no time,' I assured her, but Mama wailed even more loudly.

'What is it?' I asked, feeling suddenly chilled as I looked at Papa's grim expression. I could see that Noelle was trembling.

'They found Rachel,' Papa told me, his brow furrowed and his eyes full of sorrow. 'The soldiers questioned me briefly – asked if I'd known anything about the Jew up at Violet's school. They've obviously been busy searching all the houses in St Ouen, including the schools. They found her in the attics.'

'What will happen?' I asked, distraught.

'She's been arrested. I'm afraid she'll almost certainly end up being transferred to Europe. To a concentration camp.'

'And Sybil? And her parents?'

Papa rubbed his forehead. I heard a catch in his voice as he spoke. 'Them, too.'

'Oh, Papa!'

'The worst of it is the irony. Rachel's been terrified about being deported from Jersey ever since the Germans got here. But we don't know for sure that would have ever happened if she'd just tried to carry on as normal, though her fear was understandable. By feigning suicide and hiding with Sybil and her family she's guaranteed deportation not just for herself but for Sybil and her parents as well. The *Kommandant* is unlikely to show much mercy after they disobeyed his order.'

'What a dreadful mess!'

'Yes,' said Papa, and he reached for his pipe. 'What a dreadful, dreadful mess.'

Chapter Thirty-One

JERSEY, DECEMBER 2016

LIBERTY

'I don't think that supper could have been more perfect!' Libby declared as she threw down her napkin. 'And fancy you all cooking my favourite. Especially when Dad doesn't even like crab.' Libby smiled, raising her glass to Henry.

For some reason, Henry was looking a little twitchy. He kept glancing at his watch. She tried to remember what event he had on tonight. Whatever. She didn't have to think about it. All she had to do was actually enjoy being in the company of her family. 'Would it be pushing my luck to suggest a board game after supper?' Libby asked, and Liam groaned.

'Okay,' he agreed. 'But only if we get to choose which one.'

There was a race from the table as the three children dashed off to the old toy cupboard to find a game as if they were little kids again. Libby ignored the inevitable squabbles and squeezed Henry's hand.

'Thank you, Hen,' she said, but he still looked distracted.

'I'm just going to get some more coal for the fire,' he said, dashing into the sitting room to pick up the scuttle and then rushing through the utility room to the shed by the back door. Libby could hear the coal being scooped up and thrust into the scuttle.

'Have you decided?' she asked, turning to the kids.

'Yep, Pictionary!' Amy said, waving the game in triumph. That one had clearly been her choice.

'Excellent, let's go through and get started, then. Dad's just getting some coal in for the fire.'

They left the clearing up and trooped through to the sitting room, which was still looking dazzlingly pretty. Libby sat down cross-legged by the fire while Amy bossily arranged the game and reminded everyone of the rules.

'We'll go first,' she said. She'd craftily teamed up with Milo, who was a brilliant artist. But just then, the back door slammed and Libby heard voices. Then the door from the kitchen opened.

'Mum!' she yelled, hopping up. 'Dad! What on earth are you doing here?' Libby rushed towards her parents and embraced them both at the same time so they were clasped into a group hug.

Henry appeared from behind them with the coal, grinning from ear to ear. 'They were meant to be here hours ago but the plane was delayed due to crosswinds!'

'It was a bit bumpy!' Tink admitted. She was in her 'travel wear' – not a tracksuit but smart trousers with a fitted jacket and a polka-dot scarf tied at a rakish angle around her neck. Tink lived in the hope of being upgraded to business class.

'But . . . But what about the cats? You said after you went on that cruise that you'd never leave them again. You missed them too much!'

'But the cruise was two weeks. We're just here for a few days. And we've managed to get a lovely lady to come and house-sit so they can be in the comfort of their own home. We've left them each a stocking and they weren't too put out! Now, do I spy champagne?' asked Tink, clocking Libby's glass.

'We've already drunk the first bottle but there's more in the garage. Henry and the children stocked up on everything today. We're all set. Now I realise why you were so twitchy all through supper,' Libby said, turning to Henry.

'I was so worried they wouldn't get in. There's snow forecast for tomorrow and once that sets in, no one's going to be getting in or out. I thought I heard a taxi outside, that's why I went to get some coal!'

'Oh, Henry, thank you so much. What an amazing surprise!'

'I'm just glad you think it's a nice one,' said Alf. 'I'm always wary of surprises. You can't always be sure how they'll be received.'

'Well, you didn't need to worry about this one. I'm over the moon! Now come and sit down and have a drink.'

Drinks were brought through by the newly helpful Liam, while the other two children enjoyed hugs and chit-chat with their grandparents. Milo was always more receptive to Tink than anyone else. Libby was just clearing Pictionary out of the way (they'd save it for tomorrow) when she felt a tap on her shoulder.

'You okay, Dad?' she asked, turning round.

'I just wondered how things were going with Stella.'

'Not good. There's lots to tell you.'

'Oh dear! Have you finished the journal?'

'No, I've been so ridiculously busy, but I'm nearly there.'

'Well, see if you can finish it tonight.'

'Why?'

'Let's just say there's another surprise in store tomorrow.'

Chapter Thirty-Two

Jersey, December 1941

Queenie

Christmas Day began with yet another drama. There was a battering at the back door at two o'clock in the morning. We were all terrified, thinking the Germans were back to search the house again, but there stood Tommy, his cap in his hand and in a terrible state.

'Can your wife help?' Tommy asked Papa. 'She's a midwife, isn't she? It's the baby. Stéphanie brought him home from hospital because the new bloody curfew meant she couldn't feed him in the night. But he's failing, eh. Can your good lady help us? Please?'

'I'll do my best,' Mama said, tying her dressing-gown belt as she rushed into the kitchen, her hair down to her waist: I hadn't realised just how long it had got. She wears it in a bun every single day. 'Let me just get some clothes on,' she said.

'Mama, the curfew,' I said, following her up the stairs, but she wasn't going to take any notice of that. Before she left, though, she turned to Noelle. 'We need your German friend,' she said. 'See if you can get word to him. Tell him Tommy's address.'

After Mama left, I turned to Noelle. 'Do you know where he's billeted?' I asked.

'Of course,' she answered. I begged Noelle to let me go with her but she wouldn't let me. Papa and I were left at home wondering how on earth Mama and Noelle were getting on. At quarter past seven in the morning, with the pair of us still sitting at the kitchen table, Noelle returned with Wolfgang in tow.

'Come in, come in,' said Papa, and I'd never seen him so welcoming towards Wolfgang. 'What's the news?' he asked.

'The baby needed to be in hospital,' Wolfgang replied.

'Oh, Papa, Wolfgang was so wonderful!' gushed Noelle, unable to contain herself. 'He drove Stéphanie and the baby to hospital and stayed to help, then gave orders that Stéphanie was to be found a bed there so she can stay and feed the baby until he's better.'

'Is he going to be all right?' I asked. 'The baby?'

'Thanks to Wolfgang, yes!' Noelle answered, her cheeks flushed with pride.

'And Mama?' asked Papa, clearly worried.

'Oh, she's fine,' answered Noelle. 'She stayed with Tommy to make sure he was all right. She didn't want to risk returning home during curfew, so she'll probably be home any minute.'

Papa stood up and blow me down with a feather if he didn't shake Wolfgang's hand!

'You've been so kind. Thank you. I should like to ask you to stay to eat with us today.'

Wolfgang's eyes filled with tears. 'Thank you. That would be very decent of you. It will be very special for me, too, because, I must tell you, tomorrow I leave Jersey.'

Noelle turned to him, horrified. 'What? But you never said!'

'I only found out yesterday. I'm afraid I am needed elsewhere.'

'Where?' Noelle asked. The answer was the worst she could have imagined.

'Russia.'

Later in the morning, and with Mama safely home, we all got ourselves ready for church, then congregated in the kitchen. I had my favourite red velvet dress on, which I bring out every year. We had the wireless on and were listening to the BBC playing festive tunes.

'Today's a day to be celebrated, no matter what,' Mama said, checking the clock on the wall above the range. 'Right, everyone ready for church?'

'Just need my scarf,' I replied, racing upstairs to grab it. I paused at the window on the landing. A mist hung over the water, like a magic carpet, but – while chilly at that moment – it looked like it would soon lift to produce a day as mild as spring. Outside, as I walked to church the air felt heavy and moist.

'Funny weather for Christmas,' Mama complained as we walked to church. 'I like it a bit crisper than this.'

'Nothing's normal at the moment,' Papa replied, taking his pipe out of his mouth to speak. The heavy scent of tobacco mixed with the moist air made me feel strange and breathless.

The service that ensued matched the general atmosphere in the parish: sombre. More like Good Friday than Christmas Day. The vicar had even chosen the more melancholy Christmas carols to sing, including my favourite, 'In the Bleak Midwinter'. We sang, most of us trying not to cry:

In the bleak midwinter, frosty wind made moan,
Earth stood hard as iron, water like a stone;

Snow had fallen, snow on snow, snow on snow,
In the bleak midwinter, long ago.

I looked around me. Papa, with his lovely moustache, his eyes sad but his chin proud; Noelle, with a heartbroken look about her – no doubt thinking of Wolfgang and whether she'd ever see him again after today; Mama, singing her heart out – determined not to be beaten. Beside Mama were Odette and Sabine, looking smart and polished. Across the aisle were the Ecobichons, the twins with ribbons in their hair and looking uncomfortable in their best coats, fidgeting and squabbling. Behind them I spotted Ivy, Mary Jane's mother, though there was no sign of Mary Jane. In the pew behind me, I could hear Diane trilling away, her voice angelic. And then Tommy – not singing at all but clearly there to pray for his little grandson.

The volume in the church increased as we bellowed out the last verse:

What can I give Him, poor as I am?
If I were a shepherd, I would bring a lamb;
If I were a Wise Man, I would do my part;
Yet what I can I give Him: give my heart.

The mist had mostly cleared as we piled out of church and, like the day, our moods brightened as thoughts turned to Christmas lunch.

Wolfgang had attended a different service and when he arrived back at the farmhouse he asked no questions about the pork. Contrary to Mama's concerns, we feasted like kings for the first time in a long while. Mama had even managed to make us *des mèrveil'yes* (Jersey Wonders) for pudding – I've never known sugar taste that good!

After the meal, we lit candles and listened to 'Beautiful Jersey' on the gramophone and then played parlour games in the living room as the afternoon started to darken, teaching Wolfgang how to play Consequences and Charades. Then, at four o'clock, there was the King's Speech, so we huddled around the wireless in the kitchen to listen to it.

'You must make the most of this,' Wolfgang warned us. 'There is talk that the next reprisal will be a ban on all wirelesses.'

We listened, enraptured, as the King spoke of 'our one great family'. As he called on us all to face the coming year with 'courage, strength and good heart to overcome the perils that lie ahead', we all had to dab at our eyes with hankies, even Wolfgang. After that, though, the BBC played 'Winter Wonderland' and, oh my, did that cheer us all up! As soon as it finished, we were all singing.

Sleigh bells ring, are you listening,
In the lane, snow is glistening
A beautiful sight
We're happy tonight,
Walking in a winter wonderland . . .

There was a knock at the door. As usual, I felt dread rise within me. I jumped up first and, after taking a deep breath, opened it.

'Mary Jane!' I said, surprised. 'What are you doing here?'

The girl looked a fright. She was pale as a ghost and doubled over. She looked at me and, at once, understanding dawned.

'Mama!' I called. 'Come quickly!'

Papa and Wolfgang discreetly slunk off to milk the cows while Mama, Noelle and I helped Mary Jane up the stairs and laid her on the bed in the *cabinet*.

'Where's your mother?' Mama asked.

'She's had a bit to drink. She got some from Bob on the black market and she's not used to it now. She's gone to bed.'

Mama sighed and plumped up a pillow for the girl. 'How bad are the cramps?' she asked.

'Really bad!' whispered Mary Jane. Mama stroked her hair and issued instructions to Noelle and me. Noelle was ordered to fetch a hot-water bottle and a cold cloth for Mary Jane's brow, while I was to let her grab hold of my hand.

'I'm losing it, aren't I?' she asked, tears rolling down her face. 'The baby? They took me in for questioning yesterday morning and, I don't know, maybe it was the stress of it . . .'

'Yes, my love, I'm sorry,' said Mama. 'There's nothing we can do but keep you comfortable. It'll all be over soon.'

Mary Jane closed her eyes. When she opened them again, they were wild. 'It's God's retribution,' she said, her mouth downturned, bearing her crooked bottom teeth. 'For what I did!'

Mama and I looked at each other.

'What you did?' asked Mama, gently.

'God forgive me!' she croaked. 'I can't keep it in any longer! You know what I did, don't you? I can see it in your eyes.' Mama and I exchanged another glance. 'I don't know how I'm going to live with myself . . . You know, don't you? I did such a terrible thing!'

My prime suspect: my first instinct had been right. The poor girl. Had the Grim One wanted her to get rid of the baby? Had there been a dreadful row about it? How premeditated had the murder been? I was desperate to know more but Mama hushed her.

'Now, now,' she said. 'Don't think about that business for now. Tomorrow, Mary Jane. Tomorrow we can talk.'

Chapter Thirty-Three

JERSEY, DECEMBER 2016

LIBERTY

'Where are we going?' Libby laughed, as she and Alf strolled along the lanes of L'Etacq. It was blowing a hoolie and Libby had to keep pulling her woolly hat down to stop it flying off. It was icy cold, too, and the sky and sea merged together, both a gun-metal grey.

'Nearly there,' promised Alf.

'Oh, the farmhouse!' smiled Libby as they approached their old home, right beside the beach. 'I haven't walked past it for a while. It's looking lovely, isn't it?'

'The owners have spruced it up, apparently, ready to sell.'

'It's for sale? I had no idea.'

'Ella Coutanche told us it was about to go on the market, so I rang the estate agent's and spoke to a helpful chap called Gavin. He dropped the keys off with Henry so that we could go and have a look inside!'

'No way! Did you pretend you were interested in buying it?'

'Of course not. I explained that we used to live there and that we wanted to have a little look round – wallow in a bit of nostalgia. He couldn't have been more helpful.'

Libby smiled to herself. Just as well Gavin hadn't known whom he was helping. He might not have been quite so magnanimous. 'What a wonderful surprise!' Libby said, eager to get inside. 'But what about the owners? Aren't they living here?'

'Yes, but they're away for Christmas. Gavin said they were happy for us to look round.'

'That's kind of them. Come on, then! Let's take a look.'

It was smaller than Libby remembered, but then she'd been smaller, too, the last time she'd been in the house. Everywhere had been tastefully redone and decorated but it still retained its natural, inherent warmth. It would sell in a trice because it had that indefinable X factor: a good feeling.

Libby decided to head straight for what had always been her favourite place in the house: the window on the landing, where she'd played with her dolls as a child and then, as a teenager, curled up on the window seat with a good book or stared dreamily from the window out to sea. 'That's one thing that doesn't change,' she said, taking in the view as she sat on the cushioned seat with her knees tucked up beneath her. Alf sat down beside her.

'How do you feel, being back here?'

'Weird. I mean, it's such a lovely place, and with such an incredible feeling of peace and warmth, but it feels different. It's not home any more. I missed it so much when we first moved away but being here now has made me realise – home was actually just being with you and Mum. I'd have preferred to stay here, of course, but you managed to make Canterbury feel like home, too . . . How about you? Is it strange to be back?'

'I can't deny it. It's emotional. And you know me – I'm probably the least emotional person you know! I'm pleased we came, though.'

'It's lovely to have a moment just the two of us, as well. Dad, I finished the journal last night.'

'Aha! Then I know what you're thinking – that there's a piece of the puzzle missing.'

'I just felt a bit disappointed when I reached the final page. On the face of it, I can't see how it's going to help heal the rift between Stella and me. Why does it end so abruptly?' Libby asked. 'We just find out that Mary Jane was the murderer and then that's it . . . I was desperate to know more!'

'It's strange, isn't it? I've never worked out why she stopped the diary at that point. Perhaps she was too shocked by what Mary Jane told her the following day to want to record any of it.'

'But how do you know what Mary Jane told her?'

'Here,' said Alf, producing a couple of dog-eared sheets of writing paper from his pocket. Libby looked at it. A letter – from Wolfgang to Noelle, dated the 1st of January 1942.

My dearest Noelle,

I will not send this letter to you. I daren't risk it. And anyway, you are hardly likely to receive it. But I will keep it and – one day – I hope I will be able to give it to you in person. I suppose I am writing it to get my worries 'off my chest', as you English say.

Oh, how I miss you and your lovely island! Russia is so very, very cold and miserable. It is too awful to write about. What keep me going are thoughts of you!

I think of you all the time and pray you are still managing to keep our secret. Not for my own sake, but for yours. I know it is hard – I struggle with my conscience every day – but we both know it was not murder in cold blood. That is my worst worry now – that with time to reflect, you might consider me a murderer.

I go over and over that afternoon in my head. How might it have played out differently? I remember the show

– how good it was. I was watching you as you watched it, trying to commit your every little expression to my memory. Towards the end, I saw you frown and whisper to your mother. She nodded and you left the hall. No one seemed to notice. I remember being worried. You'd made such a good recovery from your illness, but I wanted to be sure you were all right. I made my exit, too, silent as a cat. I could see you up ahead in the road and wanted to shout out but before I had a chance, I realised there was a tall figure between us.

I saw you take a little path I'd never noticed before. The figure followed you. Now I was really worried. I picked up my pace and turned right along the pathway. It was dusk and quite misty, too, making it hard to see, but I heard your shout all right. I ran, then, cutting my hands on the brambles. By the time I reached you, he was pulling at your clothes, that randy beast.

I roared at him to get off you and he turned around and laughed at me, remember? You were sobbing and I reached towards you. I'm trying to remember what was said.

'Stop right there!' I think he barked at me, and then I saw it – the knife. A great big butcher's knife gripped in his hand.

'Where did you get that?' I asked him. We all carry small knives with us but this was a weapon that meant business.

'What is it to you?' he asked, though he couldn't resist telling me. 'I requisitioned a butcher's van from some village idiot. This beautiful knife was inside it. Aren't I lucky?' he laughed, swinging it back and forth. 'Now I

suggest you go, while I deal with this little tart here.' How his words provoked me!

I lunged towards him and he dropped the knife. We were fighting, scrabbling around in the undergrowth. He was on top of me, his hands around my throat. Do you remember? The next bit is a blur for me. All I know is that I managed to find the knife. I stuck it in his chest.

I didn't intend to kill him – you know that, don't you? But I knew at once he was going to die. We ran back to the farmhouse. You were shaking and I quickly washed my hands and left you there. You said you would play the piano, to calm your nerves.

I kissed you before I left. 'Never speak of this,' I told you.

'I promise,' you replied.

I don't think either of us slept that night. And the guilt, when they started to look for the Russian . . . I said I would come clean if they found him. I couldn't let him be punished for something I did. But then I was sent here, to Russia, and I have no idea if they've found the poor man or not. It stops me sleeping at night. That, and wondering if you're well and managing to keep our secret safe. And, most of all, whether you still love me after I killed that man.

Noelle, you are the love of my life. One day, this will be over and I hope so much that you will be my wife. I will make good what happened that night. I can never bring back a life, but I know that we can be good people, hopefully living in a good world.

Ich liebe dich. I love you.

Wolfgang.

Libby was stunned. She looked at her father.

'But . . .' Libby began.

'I know, it's shocking isn't it?'

'Self-defence . . .'

'That wouldn't have stood up, back then. They had no choice but to keep quiet.'

'Did they ever find Oleg the Russian or pin the blame on anyone else?'

'Luckily not, though the reprisals carried on for some time.'

'And what about Wolfgang and Noelle?'

'They both survived the war and married in 1946. I was born in Germany a year later.'

'What?' asked Libby, shocked. 'You mean . . . So Grandpa John wasn't your real father?'

'No. No, he wasn't. Very sadly, Wolfgang died in a motorcar accident when I was six months old. I don't remember him at all, though I have a few photographs. Noelle returned to Jersey and, after a couple of years, she remarried. Grandpa John. I took his surname and he became my father.'

'I never knew that . . . I . . . I can't quite believe it. And the rest of the family? Queenie? Obviously, Albert survived the war; I remember him as a lovely old uncle.'

'Yes – remarkably, he did. In 1943, his plane went down in enemy territory and he was taken prisoner. He was one of the survivors of Auschwitz.'

'Poor man!'

'Yes. They never had children but they led a very contented life together. Amazing, considering what poor Albert had been through. Queenie trained as a teacher, just as Albert thought she should, and many years later she ended up headmistress of the village primary school in St Ouen, as you know.'

'So how did it all end? The occupation?'

'Jersey was liberated in 1945, shortly before the entire island starved to death – once France was freed in 1944, all supplies were cut off. That was the most dreadful part of the occupation for most people. A very dark period in history. Another terrible moment was in 1942 when Hitler ordered the deportation of anyone who hadn't been born on the island – sent off to internment camps in Germany. But Liberation Day on the ninth of May, 1945, was, so I believe, the most incredible day the island has ever known. My mum and Queenie could never talk about it without needing to get a hanky out. You know about that, anyway, from our celebrations every year.'

'Yes, of course. I've always loved those parties and it was wonderful seeing Granny Noelle and Queenie enjoy them year after year when I was growing up. Not that I knew the half of it until now.' Libby paused, her brain fizzing. 'And Mary Jane? What happened to her? And if she wasn't confessing to the murder of the Grim One, what on earth *was* she confessing to?'

'She grassed on Sybil and her family about Rachel Weider. Sybil always thought the snitch was Wolfgang and that's why she held a grudge against our family, though we stupidly never explained it to you. She always believed Noelle had told Wolfgang about Rachel being hidden in the school attics and that he'd informed on Sybil's family to the *Kommandant*. The fact that he left the island on Boxing Day was, to Sybil, proof he'd been the one to grass on them. But it had nothing to do with Noelle or Wolfgang. It was Mary Jane who squealed.'

'So that's what she was confessing to? Not the murder, but her betrayal of Sybil and her family?'

'Exactly.'

'So what happened to Mary Jane, then, and how come Sybil never found out that it was her that went running to the authorities, not Wolfgang?'

'I needed my own answers to all this, too, as you can imagine, and I talked it all through with Queenie on many occasions before she died. I couldn't get any sense of out of my mum – she just wanted to forget.

'Apparently, Mary Jane was taken in for questioning on Christmas Eve morning regarding the Grim One's murder. The Germans were beginning to suspect she might have killed him, especially as they weren't having any luck finding Oleg. They were putting her under intense pressure, so she felt the need to divert their attention. Her mother, Ivy, was a cleaner at Violet's school and had let slip to Mary Jane about Rachel being hidden there. Mary Jane told the Germans. At the time, everyone assumed the school attics were searched as part of the rampage the Germans were on, trying to find the Russian. But in fact their search of the school was very specific and resulted from their questioning of Mary Jane.'

'No wonder she felt so bad. But how come Sybil never knew it was Mary Jane who grassed on the family?'

'When the island was liberated in 1945, Mary Jane was one of a number of women who were tarred and feathered for being Jerrybags during the occupation. She was chased out of Jersey – left in 1945 and never came back. By the time Sybil returned from Ravensbrück, Mary Jane was long gone and Noelle was living in Germany with Wolfgang. Sybil was a shadow of her former self when she got back, like a skeleton. Her parents had died in another camp and poor Rachel had been killed, too. She was all alone. Eventually, she married, though she and her husband didn't think they could have children to begin with. Stella was a surprise, born when Sybil was well into her forties, which is why you and Stella are the same age even though your parents are a generation apart.

'When she returned from Germany, after Wolfgang's death, Noelle tried to rekindle her friendship with Sybil but it was impossible. Sybil wouldn't tell her why, until eventually Noelle wore her down and it all poured out: how Noelle must have told Wolfgang about Rachel and how in turn he must have told the *Kommandant* before he disappeared. Sybil had no evidence about this but she was completely convinced. Noelle explained to her that it was Mary Jane who'd snitched on them but Sybil didn't believe it. The diary and Noelle's letter from Wolfgang together would have explained everything but Noelle could hardly tell Sybil about the murder, considering the promise she'd made to Wolfgang and the frame of mind Sybil was in. There was every chance she'd go to the police and Noelle would end up arrested.

'So there it was left. Sybil was convinced she was right and Noelle knew Sybil was wrong. That was when the grudge was born and it's festered ever since. No one in Jersey really spoke much of the occupation in the years that followed and plenty of grievances much like this were silently harboured. Growing up, you and Stella knew there was bad feeling but, of course, you never knew the reasoning behind it. Now, my dear girl, you know.'

'And now I have the journal and the letter,' Libby said. 'I need to talk to Stella.'

PART THREE

'LIFE APPEARS TO ME TOO SHORT TO BE
SPENT IN NURSING ANIMOSITY OR
REGISTERING WRONGS.'

From *Jane Eyre*
By Charlotte Brontë

Chapter Thirty-Four

LIBERTY

Alf and Libby returned to the Vicarage to find Henry serving up a fried lunch to Tink, Liam and Milo. Amy had gone into work but would be back by the evening.

'Just in time!' Henry said, shovelling bacon and eggs onto plates.

'Oh, wow! Just the ticket,' said Libby. 'Hen, I need to go and see Stella this afternoon. Is there any chance you could nip into town and pick up the turkey?'

'I'll do it,' offered Liam, still in helpful mode. 'Do you want to come with me, Milo?' he asked his brother, who nodded enthusiastically. 'Is there anything else anyone needs?'

'No, I don't think so, but you'd better go soon before the snow. Once the storm arrives, we need to batten down the hatches.'

'It's so exciting!' said Tink, grinning wildly. 'Actually, Liam, could you get me a nice bottle of sweet sherry while you're out? Can't hunker down without a decent sherry!'

'Certainly, Grandmama!' Liam agreed, addressing her jokily as he always had done, and, after wolfing down his food, he set off for town.

As soon as he was gone, Tink remarked, 'He seems so much more stable. It must have all been a bit of a wake-up call.'

'I think it was. It shook us all up no end. Now,' Libby said, washing down her bacon and eggs with a strong mug of tea, 'if you don't mind, I think I'd better head to Stella's.'

'Good luck!' said Henry, Tink and Alf in unison, and Libby laughed nervously.

Bundled up in her warmest coat, she set off for Stella's cottage on the Five Mile Road – the road running alongside St Ouen's Bay, five minutes from L'Etacq. She just hoped Stella wouldn't be working. She knocked on the door and a moment later Stella opened it, with Rusty jumping up and down with glee when he spotted Libby.

'Libby?' Stella said guardedly, looking perplexed. 'I'm just about to go out, I'm afraid.' She didn't look like she was going anywhere. Libby peeped past her to the kitchen and could see some mince pies that in fact looked just about ready to be popped into the Rayburn.

'Please, Stella, I only need five minutes. I've got something to show you – something to explain. It won't take long, I promise.'

Stella reluctantly opened the door and gestured to a kitchen chair. She stood, arms crossed, without offering Libby a drink, though she was supremely hospitable as a rule.

'Look, I totally understand why you were angry after everything I'm guessing your mum told you. But Dad's just lent me a journal kept by my great-aunt Queenie during the occupation. There's a letter, too. I've got them here,' Libby said, waving them. 'Stella, your mum thought Granny Noelle told her German doctor, Wolfgang, about the Jewish girl and that he then snitched on your family, didn't she? But that wasn't the case.'

'Yes, it was! And my grandparents died because of it! He might just as well have put a gun to their heads himself.'

'But it wasn't him that informed on them, Stella! It was this woman called Mary Jane. She had an affair with a really nasty German officer. The man got his comeuppance in the end, which is a whole other story . . . But Mary Jane was pregnant with his child. The Germans were questioning her about him on Christmas Eve in 1941 and, under pressure, and probably to deflect their attention, she told them about Rachel Weider being hidden in the school attics. Her mum was the cleaner at the school and had let slip to Mary Jane about Rachel. That information got Mary Jane out of a tight spot but at great cost to Rachel and your family. Wolfgang didn't have anything to do with your mum ending up in a concentration camp. Honestly, Stella.'

Stella hopped from foot to foot, her strawberry blonde curls bouncing as she looked out of the window. Libby knew her so well. Her interest had been piqued but she was a stubborn old thing. There was no point trying to push the point now. Libby got up.

'Look, Stella, I'm going to leave the journal and the letter here with you. Have a read, please, for the sake of all those years we had being friends. If you want nothing more to do with me after that, then so be it.'

Libby got up from the chair and made her way to the door. 'Stella, one more thing. You and Rusty are welcome at ours tomorrow, for Christmas Day. I'll lay a place for you. Just in case . . .'

Stella bit her lip. She looked flushed with emotion. 'Bye, Libby,' she said, and she closed the door.

Chapter Thirty-Five

Jersey, 24 December 2016

Liberty

Libby had no idea whether Stella would soften once she looked at the letter and the journal but she didn't have time to dwell on the matter, as by the time she arrived home it was nearly two o'clock and the excitement in the house was palpable. It was impossible not to get swept along by it.

'Amy!' she said, seeing her daughter chattering away to Tink at the kitchen table. 'I thought you weren't getting here till six!'

'Oh, Mum, it's so exciting! I was in the office and suddenly the snow started! The senior partner told everyone to head home, so we all grabbed our coats and bags, wished each other Merry Christmas, and then legged it to our cars. The snow's already really thick in town, so the traffic was appalling. Jonty's gone to his parents but I was just explaining to Gran that, as they're only in St Mary, he can walk to us tomorrow if needs be. It can only be a matter of time until it starts up here! I looked at the forecast and the storm's due tomorrow afternoon, so they reckon there's going to be a huge snowstorm!'

Libby smiled. She hadn't seen her daughter so animated in years. She was sporting an incongruous Christmas jumper: dark green with a rotund Father Christmas on the front, his nose a fluffy red pom-pom. Amy saw Libby clocking the unusual attire.

'It's a tradition at work,' Amy laughed. 'We always wear Christmas jumpers in the office on Christmas Eve!'

'And you?' Libby asked, spotting that Tink was adorned in a similarly garish and festive pullover.

'Oh, as soon as Amy arrived I knew I had to keep her company. Lucky I packed this one,' she said, patting her fluffy snowman sweater proudly.

'Well, I ought to join you then. I've got that one Hen gave me for Christmas last year with the Christmas pudding on it. I was never sure if the gift was ironic or not!'

'Oh, yes!' Tink exclaimed. 'You must! Nip and change and I'll make some hot chocolate. Did you notice the wreath on the door? A lady turned up with that and a lovely arrangement for the table. Oh, and Liam called. He got stuck in traffic, too, but he's made it back to St Ouen. He's got the turkey and my sherry but he's just stopped at the Splash for a beer with some friends. Milo's with him. And Henry and Dad have gone up to the church to get everything ready for Midnight Mass.'

'Okey-dokey. I've just got to wrap a few more prezzies while I'm upstairs. Give me a shout when the hot chocolate's ready.'

Libby raced up the stairs, as excited as a child. She quickly swapped her navy cowl neck for the festive jumper and set about wrapping the last of her presents. She heard Amy yelling up the stairs that the drink was ready and shoved all her wrapping paper back behind the dressing table before gathering up armfuls of presents, carefully balancing them on top of one another as she made her way down the stairs to put them under the tree. But halfway down she stopped and looked out of the window on the half-landing. It had started. She saw the flakes dancing in the wind, decent thick ones that couldn't possibly be described as snow's disappointing sister, sleet.

'It's started!' she said, bursting into the kitchen. 'The snow!'

By the time Liam, Milo, Henry and Alf returned, all at once, the ground was covered.

'Just made it!' said Henry, dusting down his waxed jacket as he entered the kitchen from the utility room, the others following behind – Liam weighed down by the turkey. 'No idea what to do about Midnight Mass. I've never had to cancel a service before. Do you think I should?'

'You can't cancel Midnight Mass!' shrieked Tink, as though she were a devout Christian, rather than someone who attended church once a year for the feel-good festive factor.

'I don't think we'll be able to drive though.'

'Then we'll walk,' said Tink, not taking any nonsense. 'It's not far. We'll take torches and wrap up warm. There's enough people living within walking distance to make it worthwhile.'

Henry went over and patted Tink's back, laughing. 'Oh, okay, then,' he agreed. 'There was me hoping for an early bath.'

Tink tutted and offered more hot chocolate but Henry decided it was about time a bottle was cracked open.

'Tell you what,' said Liam. 'Why don't I make some mulled wine?'

Everyone agreed that would be perfect and all of a sudden each of them became industrious. Henry lit the fire, while Alf brought in more logs. Tink started preparing the sprouts for the following day, and Libby set about steeping the turkey in a bath of water as suggested by her heroine, Nigella. She found an old baby bath and, after filling it with quartered oranges, salt, sugar, syrup and honey, gently lowered in the colossal bird. Meanwhile, Amy took the kitchen radio through to the sitting room and tuned it to Radio 4 so they could all listen to the carol service from King's, a family tradition that was not to be messed with. The jobs accomplished and Liam's wine mulled, they took their warm beakers through to the sitting room, where they chatted by the fire and joined in with the carols – even Milo managing an hour with the family before he slunk off to practise his drums.

Rather than cooking a heavy meal, Libby produced platters of smoked salmon on brown bread at about six o'clock and after a bit of festive television – and to while away the time until Midnight Mass – Tink suggested they play those games that only seem to be remembered once a year: Charades and the like. Milo couldn't be persuaded to join in but everyone else had a whale of a time – so much so that the clock hands quickly crept towards eleven o'clock.

'If we're walking, then we need to leave in ten minutes,' said Henry, and there was a sudden frenzy as Tink, Libby and Amy dashed upstairs to glam themselves up for the service, while Henry put the finishing touches to his sermon and Alf and Liam enjoyed one more snifter. Once she'd powdered her nose and spritzed herself liberally with perfume, Libby went to find Milo.

'Do I have to come?' he moaned.

'Course you don't . . . But it'd be lovely for Dad – to know we're all there with him. You decide. We're leaving in two minutes.'

Those two minutes were filled by everyone piling on coats and finding wellington boots. Eventually, they all congregated by the front door.

'Ready?' asked Henry. Libby realised Milo hadn't emerged from his room and felt a small pang, but she'd learned from raising the older two that teenagers didn't respond well to strong-arming. She was about to lock the front door when she saw a face on the other side of the glazed window.

'Wait for me!' It was Milo. Libby couldn't help herself – she pulled him into a hug.

They left, all holding on to each other for dear life, heading in the direction of the bells.

The service was surprisingly full and had that indefinable magic to it that Midnight Mass always seemed to offer. Henry put on a sterling performance and, feeling weary now, the group began the trudge home through the snow. Henry, Tink and the children ploughed on ahead, while Libby hung back with Alf.

'I keep thinking about the characters in the journal,' she said. 'What happened to Oleg? Was he ever discovered?'

'No, amazingly not,' said Alf. 'The hidey-hole under the floorboards did the trick during the big search and he stayed hidden with Mrs Lucas until the liberation. He returned to his family in Russia after the war but he stayed in contact with Mrs Lucas who – incidentally – received a bravery award for hiding Oleg for all those years. As did Sybil, for everything she did for Rachel.

'Mrs Lucas left her house to Oleg, eventually, when she died. Oleg was an old man himself by then but he did move to Jersey and spent the last year of his life here. I believe his wife had died by then and his children had married and made lives for themselves. He loved Jersey so much, despite what he'd been through. You might have seen him in L'Etacq – he went for a swim in the sea every day, no matter what the weather was like!'

'Oh, gosh, yes! That lovely old chap! I know exactly who you mean. And what about Diane?'

'She was one of the victims of Hitler's deportation order in 1942. She wasn't local, though her husband had been, so she ended up in an internment camp in a place called Biberach in Germany. But after the war she was reunited with her children in England and she ended up marrying the pilot she'd met in Jersey! Remember? The one she swam out to rescue in St Brelade's Bay? They found each other and Diane and the children moved to make a life with him wherever he was from. Up north, I think.'

'And Tommy?'

'He continued with his butcher's business till the day he died. His little grandson survived and turned into a strapping young lad. He took over the family business when Tommy passed away. It's still going strong today, though it's in town now – in the market. *Le Brun & Sons.*'

'That's the one I use! That's where our turkey's from! I feel like I miss them all,' Libby said. 'All those characters.'

'Most of them are long gone by now,' Alf replied. 'It's incredible to think what they all had to endure . . .'

'It's hard to believe it wasn't even that long ago. We needlessly over-complicate life nowadays, don't we? Me, especially. I've decided I'm going to make it my New Year's resolution to simplify more and worry less.'

Alf smiled. 'How did it go with Stella?'

'Dad, I don't think she's going to forgive me, regardless of the letter and the journal. But I've asked her to lunch tomorrow. If she doesn't turn up, then I'll know that's it.'

'She'll be there,' said Alf. 'You mark my words.'

Chapter Thirty-Six

Jersey, 25 December 2016

Liberty

It was Christmas morning and Libby leapt out of bed to open the curtains. The whole of L'Etacq was white, even the beach. Although it was chilly by the window, she couldn't drag herself away from the view.

'We'll be walking to church again,' she remarked to Henry, who grunted and turned over, clearly not ready to start the day. But his peace was disturbed half an hour later when, just as they'd done as little children, all three kids burst through to Libby and Henry's room and everyone began opening their stockings. Libby wondered how many more years they'd continue to insist on them, then felt a pang of sadness when she realised that, by the following Christmas, Amy would be married, and her stocking would no longer be Libby's responsibility.

As tradition in their house dictated, after stockings they trooped downstairs for breakfast and then opened a couple of presents each before getting ready for church. While Henry and the children exclaimed at the treasures they hurriedly unwrapped, Libby slowly selected two gifts nestling under the tree, one of which was from Alf and piqued Libby's interest as usually such presents came from both her parents.

'Are you opening one of the ones from me?' Henry asked.

'Yes, this one!' She ripped open the wrapping and found a copy of *Country Life*.

'It's a year's subscription,' said Henry. 'To fuel your property lust!'

'You know me too well!' Libby laughed. 'Thank you so much! I'm going to make the time to settle down and read it from cover to cover every month.'

'Dad, I'm going to open this one from you now!' Libby then called out to Alf, who trooped into the sitting room with a tray of mugs.

She tore at the paper. 'A painting of our old farmhouse! Oh, it's beautiful!' she said. The picture, framed in light oak, was painted with vibrantly coloured acrylics and the likeness to her childhood home was astounding.

'Do you recognise the artist?' Alf asked, offering Libby a mug of tea. She propped the picture up and took the drink, then looked again at the painting, squinting.

'I don't think I do,' she said. 'Though they're very talented.'

Alf pointed towards Milo, who blushed bright red.

'No way! You commissioned Milo! But this must have taken you weeks, sweetheart! And it's not your usual style at all!'

'Months,' Milo admitted. 'It was one of the reasons I kept sneaking off to my room. I wasn't *just* being a grumpy teenager. My art teacher's got me into experimenting with acrylics.'

Libby didn't know who to hug first but before she had a chance to cuddle either of them, she found herself leapt upon by Tink, who'd just opened her present to discover the grey cape she'd coveted so much. 'You sneaky girl!' she laughed. 'I adore it! I shall never take it off!'

Then, in a repeat of the night before, there was a rush for the bathroom as everyone readied themselves for church at once and then piled out of the front door into the snow. The Vicarage pew was reserved for Libby and the family and they immediately filled it. A moment later Jonty joined them and everyone squeezed up for him.

Henry's service was thoroughly enjoyable: a nice short sermon and the most rousing of Christmas carols. Remarkably, he'd even chosen 'In the Bleak Midwinter' as the offertory hymn. Remembering Queenie's journal entry for Christmas Day, Libby felt a lump in her throat as she imagined her ancestors standing in the very same church singing the exact same hymn seventy-five years before, with absolutely no idea how their future would turn out. Nearly all the characters had been at church – Queenie, Noelle, Mama, Papa, Sabine, Diane, the Ecobichons and Tommy . . . She recalled Queenie describing how, aside from Tommy, who'd been busy praying for his grandson, they'd all bravely sung their hearts out to the melancholy carol and yet how terrifying life must have been for them at that moment in time.

They were home in good time for lunch, which, for the first time ever, was a joint effort. Libby was just about to serve up when the doorbell rang.

'Hen! Can you take over? I'll get the door,' she said.

Just as Alf had predicted, there at the door was Stella, with Rusty pulling at his lead. He panted with joy when he saw Libby. The wind was whistling outside and the snow was whirling about in circles, drifts quickly building.

'Stella! You shouldn't be out in this! Come in!'

Stella took a step inside the hallway and Libby closed the front door. 'It wasn't an easy walk. Here,' Stella said, passing Libby a brown paper bag. Libby looked inside.

'Jersey Wonders! They're still warm! Did you make them?' Libby asked, astonished.

Stella nodded. 'I took the class. You remember? We had it booked for our franniversary. I decided to go along anyway so I could make them for the Refuge. Not that I could get there this morning in this snow. I'd just been to the class when I saw you in the coffee shop the other day. It was lovely learning how to make them but, Libby, I've never felt so lonely in my life.'

Libby didn't know what to say. Was Stella saying she wanted to make up?

'I haven't read the diary or the letter,' Stella continued, hopping from foot to foot and pushing her strawberry blonde curls out of her eyes. 'Not yet, anyway. But by some weird coincidence there was this article in the paper yesterday. I don't know if you saw it. It was about a man who'd been deported in 1942 and spent three years in an internment camp in Germany. Wurzach, the place was called – now Bad Wurzach – and, in spite of everything he'd been through, he was instrumental in the twinning of St Helier with the town where he'd been interned.

'It was such an incredible act of reconciliation. I read the article and I felt my cheeks burn with shame. He bore no grudge at all. And I thought to myself – here's me bearing a grudge when I don't even have my facts straight. Libby, I believe what you've told me about your grandmother and her German doctor and that woman called Mary Jane. But even if I didn't, it would be criminal of me to throw away our friendship based on something that happened so long ago, during a period of history I can't even begin to imagine. I'll never forget what my family had to endure but I realise now that the past needs to be laid to rest – for my own sake, if for no other reason. I think it was all tied up with my grief to start with and then, stubborn mule that I am, I just couldn't let it go. And some of the things I've said since have been horrible. I'm so sorry, Libs,' Stella said, offering her hand.

Libby thought back – to the occupation days she'd managed to catch a glimpse of through Queenie's journal and to the last few weeks when she and Stella had been at war themselves. In so many ways, the two periods in time couldn't have been more in contrast, but the feelings all those characters experienced back in 1941 were no different from those that she and Stella and billions of other people felt today: sorrow, joy, boredom, stress, anger, grief, love and – above all else – hope. Hope for the future.

'So am I,' said Libby, and she took Stella's hand.

Epilogue

After lunch, with everyone holding their stomachs and begging not to be given any more food, the lights began to flicker. They were all squeezed round the dining table at one end of the sitting room. The table had been passed down the generations and was so fragile it was liable to collapse should anyone lean on it, but so far it had stood up to the Christmas lunch. Someone had put on the TV so they wouldn't miss the Queen's Speech.

'Uh-oh!' said Henry, taking a slug of red wine. 'Think it's time we lit the candles. The forecasters were spot on, weren't they?'

Libby got up and went to the window, pushing it open.

'Mum, it's freezing! What are you doing?' Amy complained, but Libby stuck her head out. The sky was almost black and the wind was howling, the drifts of snow nearly as high as the window now. There was something exhilarating about breathing in the ice-cold, wintery gusts, knowing that, as soon as she wanted to, she could secure the latch and retreat to the warmth and comfort of her home. She shivered and closed the window quickly, then pulled the curtains across. She dashed into the kitchen to fetch the matches and diligently made her way around the room, lighting the many candles that were dotted about. She'd just lit the very last one when the lights flickered again, then went out.

Tink squealed in delight and they all abandoned the dining table to join Rusty by the fire, each one of them – even Milo – seemingly relishing the peace that resulted from the sudden shutdown of the TV. They sat companionably for a moment, each cradling a drink, until Henry broke the spell.

'I propose a toast!' he said, raising his glass. 'To Christmas. To family. To friends. And – most of all – to peace.'

Their glasses clinked, the sound like the ringing of Christmas bells.

Author's Note and Acknowledgments

Though this novel has been based upon extensive historical research, it is in no way intended to be an authority on life during the German occupation of Jersey and I have allowed myself a certain amount of artistic licence – especially regarding the murder and the repercussions that followed, as well as the concealment of Rachel. This scenario was unlikely to have arisen until after the deportation orders of 1942 but I was keen to include this important part of the occupation within the novel.

I would like to thank everyone I've thanked in my previous novels, most especially my husband, Dan, my daughters, Ruby and Iris, all of my extended family, my loyal readers, and everyone at Amazon Publishing (particularly Sammia Hamer, Victoria Pepe, Emilie Marneur, Katie Green, John Marr, Nick de Somogyi and Bekah Graham). I would also like to thank the following people who assisted with my research: Lorna Lambourne, Sarah and Graham Boxall, Brian and Hazel Vibert, Mark Grieve, Michael John Michel, Hamish Marett-Crosby, Matthew Price (BBC Radio Jersey), Colin Isherwood (Occupation Society), Mrs Charlesworth (Les Landes School) and Carla McDonald (lighthouse information).

Bibliography

'A Heroine Remembered', *Jersey Evening Post* (21 November 2016), http://jerseyeveningpost.com/news/2016/11/21/a-heroine-remembered/.

Brown, Mike, *Christmas on the Home Front* (Gloucestershire: Sutton Publishing, 2004).

Bunting, Madeleine *The Model Occupation: The Channel Islands under German Rule, 1940–1945* (London: HarperCollins, 1995).

Faramus, Anthony *Journey into Darkness* (London: Grafton Books, 1990).

Harris, Leo, *A Boy Remembers* (Jersey: Apache Guides Limited, 2000).

Hillsdon, Sonia (ed.), *Jersey Occupation Remembered* (Norwich: Jarrold and Sons Ltd, 1986).

Keane, Mauyen *Hello, Is It All Over?* (Eire: Ababuna, 1984).

Le Boutillier, Marianne, *The King behind the Picture: The Story of a Boy during the German Occupation of Jersey* (Bradford on Avon, Wiltshire: Ex Libris Press, 2013).

Le Roux, Grace, 'Guiding During the German Occupation 1940–1945', www.girlguidingjersey.org.je/history/war-years

Le Ruez, Nan, *Jersey Occupation Diary* (St Helier: Seaflower Books, 1994).

Lewis, John, *A Doctor's Occupation* (London: Corgi, 1982).

McLoughlin, Roy *Living with the Enemy: What Really Happened* (Jersey: Starlight Publishing, 1996).

Mayne, Richard, (ed.), *Channel Islands Occupied: Unique Pictures of the Nazi Rule* (Norwich: Jarrold and Sons Ltd, 1978).

Nettles, John, *Jewels and Jackboots: Hitler's British Channel Islands* (Jersey: Channel Island Publishing & Jersey War Tunnels, 2012).

Pocock, H. R. S. (ed.), *The Memoirs of Lord Coutanche* (London: Phillimore & Co. Ltd, 1975).

Rubery, Joanna, 'The Language of Jersey: Little Toads and the Glove of a Queen', http://blog.oxforddictionaries.com/2013/08/jersey-shore/

Sanders, Paul *The British Channel Islands Under German Occupation, 1940–1945* (Jersey: Jersey Heritage Trust and Société Jersiaise, 2005).

Sinel, L. P. (ed.), *The German Occupation of Jersey: A Diary of Events from June 1940 to June 1945* (London: Howard Baker, 1969).

Tregenza, Liz, *Style Me Vintage. 1940s: An Inspirational Guide to the Hair, Make-up and Fashions of the 40s* (London: Pavilion, 2015).

Watkins, Simon, *Hitler's British Islands* (Jersey: Channel Island Publishing, 2000).

About the Author

Photo © 2016 Vix Atkinson

Rebecca Boxall was born in 1977 in East Sussex, where she grew up in a bustling vicarage always filled with family, friends and parishioners. She now lives by the sea in Jersey with her husband and two children. She read English at the University of Warwick before training as a lawyer and also studied Creative Writing with The Writers Bureau. She is the author of *Christmas at the Vicarage* and *Home for Winter*.

13159154R00129

Printed in Great Britain
by Amazon